# UNRAVELED
## TAMI BOYER

# UNRAVELED

This is a work of fiction. All of the characters, names, incidents, organizations, and dialogue in this novel are either the products of the author's imagination or are used fictitiously.

iUniverse books may be ordered through booksellers or by contacting:

iUniverse
1663 Liberty Drive
Bloomington, IN 47403
www.iuniverse.com
1-800-Authors (1-800-288-4677)

Because of the dynamic nature of the Internet, any web addresses or links contained in this book may have changed since publication and may no longer be valid. The views expressed in this work are solely those of the author and do not necessarily reflect the views of the publisher, and the publisher hereby disclaims any responsibility for them.

Any people depicted in stock imagery provided by Getty Images are models, and such images are being used for illustrative purposes only. Certain stock imagery © Getty Images.

ISBN: 978-1-5320-4047-4 (sc)
ISBN: 978-1-5320-4046-7 (e)

Library of Congress Control Number: 2018901947

Print information available on the last page.

iUniverse rev. date: 02/06/2018

# THE TWINS

This morning Tom awoke a bit earlier than usual. *Today is going to be a busy, stressful day.* He decided to get to it. Grabbing the coffee out of the cupboard, he turned and tripped over Cindy, the five-year-old collie who had followed him from her bed on the floor of their bedroom. As the container flew from his hand, Tom struggled to gain control of it and slipped on the kitchen tile, watching the coffee spill as he fell to the floor.

Rising to his feet, he laughed and said, "If this is how my day is going to go, I will go back to bed."

Tom decided not to start the day with a negative attitude. He gave Cindy a pat and readied the coffeepot.

He heard running water coming from the bathroom. Brenda, his wife, was awake and changing for breakfast.

Tom began to think about the past two months, how much his wife had been through, and how much he loved her. *This day has to go well.* Tom looked to the ceiling and said, "Please, God. Please let this day be the best day of our lives. Brenda needs this—she really needs this."

At the end of November, Tom and Brenda had found out they were going to be parents. What a joyous Thanksgiving they celebrated with family and friends. Just days after the doctor confirmed the pregnancy, they began working on the nursery.

Everything seemed to be falling into place for them, but right before Christmas, something went wrong. Brenda telephoned Tom at work and asked him to come home right away. There was something wrong, and she needed to go to the hospital.

Tom rushed home and took Brenda to the emergency room. He sped and ran red lights for the entire fifteen-minute drive.

Once they arrived, she was immediately admitted for tests. The doctors informed Tom and Brenda that the pregnancy had terminated itself—and they could no longer have children.

Brenda was given a pill to help her pass the terminated pregnancy. She stayed that evening in the hospital, and Tom slept in the chair next to her bed.

Brenda became depressed, spending long hours in bed and not eating for days on end. She grew controlling and mean and said hateful things to almost anyone who crossed her path. She was nothing like the girl he had fallen in love with. He no longer knew her.

Their marriage was beginning to show signs of wear. Brenda and Tom were in trouble. Wanting to save their marriage, the two began attending couple's therapy with the church minister.

After two months of therapy, twice a week, Brenda and Tom were getting their marriage back on track. With joy and love for each other in their hearts, the happy couple decided to adopt a baby.

*Today, we will find out if our prayers and dreams have been answered. Today, we will find out if we will be able to grow our family.*

Brenda entered the kitchen and kissed Tom on the cheek. He looked at her, took note of her beauty, and thought of his love for her. He would do anything for her. He was a loyal and faithful husband.

He handed her a cup of coffee and brushed the hair from her face. Looking out the picture window, Tom could see the snow falling. The morning sun was casting a beautiful glow on the snow. *Such marvelous sight*, Tom thought. *This is a good sign.*

They arrived at the adoption agency a few minutes early. Brenda took a seat in the waiting area while Tom checked in with the receptionist. The young, blonde, big-busted woman behind the desk informed Tom that Mrs. Edwards would be right out. Brenda was fidgety and very nervous. Tom put his hand on her knee and assured her everything would be okay.

Mrs. Edwards opened the door and asked them to step inside and sit down, greeting them joyfully and smiling. Tom hoped she was as nice as she appeared to be.

Mrs. Edwards owned and ran a dairy farm with her husband, Sylvester, outside Bakersfield. The farm had been in their family for generations. Tom grew up drinking milk from that very farm. *Another good sign*, he thought to himself.

Mrs. Edwards informed Tom and Brenda that their paperwork had been processed and approved. "The agency may have babies for you."

Brenda said, "Don't you mean *a* baby?"

Mrs. Edwards replied, "No, dear. I mean babies." There were fraternal twin boys available for adoption immediately. It seemed they were born to a mother of four who was recently divorced. She told the couple the agency would like the twins to go directly to a happy new home—from the hospital versus foster care or an orphanage.

Tom and Brenda were overwhelmed with the thought of two babies. He thought, *Can we handle two tiny babies at one time?*

Mrs. Edwards suggested they take some time to think about adopting the twins and asked Brenda and Tom to call her the next day by five o'clock.

Tom and Brenda agreed and shook her hand before leaving the office. The walk to the car was quiet; they both had a lot on their minds.

When Tom and Brenda arrived home, she put on some tea. The couple sat down at the table with pad and paper and wrote down the pros and cons of adopting twin boys.

Three hours later, it was decided the boys would be a welcomed addition to the family.

Tom and Brenda lay in bed and stared at the ceiling. Anticipation and excitement about becoming parents was the cause of their restlessness. They thought about all the things that needed to be done, immediately, with the twins coming home.

Brenda telephoned Mrs. Edwards the following morning to let her know they would be adopting the boys.

Mrs. Edwards was thrilled and offered her assistance in any way to the couple. She told Brenda that she and Tom were to meet her in the reception area at the hospital the next morning at ten for the twins' discharge.

Excitement was building within Brenda. She was looking forward to becoming a new mother, yet she was a little sad. She was still mourning the loss of her baby from months before. The new additions would surely help her fill the hole in her heart.

Brenda worked all day on finishing the nursery. It had almost been finished when Brenda lost the baby back in December, so she knew she could have it ready by the end of the day. There really wasn't much left to do. Tom's mom dropped off a second crib that morning along with a box of baby blankets and sheets.

When Tom arrived home from work, Brenda told him about the time and place where they were to meet Mrs. Edwards.

Tom asked Brenda if she had thought about names for the twins.

She replied, "Yes, Donnie and Dillon."

He hugged his wife with excitement and shouted, "Donnie and Dillon it is!"

After another sleepless night, Tom got out of bed and started the coffee. He was very careful not to fall over Cindy. He said, "No time for messes and confusion today with the boys coming home."

Brenda came into the kitchen in her pajamas. She sat down at the table, placed her hand on his, and asked, "Are you sure you want to go through with this? Twins are a handful, Tom. We need to be sure because there is no going back."

Tom touched her face and replied softly, "Yes, dear. I am excited about our new family. There are so many wonderful times ahead of us."

Brenda sighed with relief, and they sat in silence for the remainder of breakfast. The strange look on Brenda's face puzzled Tom, but he decided not to ask.

The enthusiastic new parents arrived at the hospital with flowers for Mrs. Edwards and stuffed animals for Donnie and Dillon. The bears had brilliant blue bows around their necks. One bow was light blue, and the other was navy blue. Brenda told Tom they needed to be able to tell which bear belonged to which boy.

Mrs. Edwards was waiting for Tom and Brenda in the reception area. She was grinning from ear to ear. She truly was a wonderful woman, and Tom and Brenda thanked her again for her help and support. Brenda presented Mrs. Edwards with the flowers, and she started to cry when she saw them. She led Tom and Brenda down the hall to a private room where the new family could get acquainted before the babies were released.

The room was decorated with blue balloons and streamers. There were two gift baskets filled with diapers, powder, and other essentials. Brenda looked at the bassinets in front of the large bay windows, observing the gurgles and cooing. Peering into the first bassinet, she laid her eyes on the second twin. This little angel was born five minutes after the first twin, who was waiting to meet his parents in the second bassinet. She looked at his soft blond hair. He looked like an angel. He had the biggest, brightest blue eyes she had ever seen. She began to cry—what a sight he was! Brenda named him Donnie, blew him a kiss, and turned to the second bassinet. Dillon had brown hair and somber green eyes. She felt an immediate connection with Dillon. She was filled with love and admiration for him. Brenda didn't feel anything for Donnie. It was if he didn't exist. She took Dillon into her arms, he smelled like baby powder and lotion. She had never experienced anything like it. Brenda began to cry again.

Tom stepped up to the first bassinet with tears in his eyes. He looked down at Donnie and sighed. He thought, *Thank you, God. Thank you for these babies. It doesn't get much better than this.* He picked up Donnie as tears fell from his eyes. He kissed the tiny cheek of this precious baby and wondered why Brenda had not picked up Donnie too. Tom noticed another strange look on Brenda's face but decided to overlook it. *She is probably overwhelmed.* He was immediately filled with love for his new family.

Mrs. Edwards was a great help in getting the boys buckled into the back seat of Tom's Pontiac. As a mother of six, she made it look pretty easy. She hugged Brenda and Tom, wishing them the best, and handed Tom a piece of paper with her telephone number. "Please call me if you two ever need help with anything. We would love to have you and the boys over for a picnic."

Tom and Brenda thanked her again and closed the doors.

With the boys secure, the new family headed home. The drive down old 55 was beautiful. Looking out at the fields covered with snow, Tom saw a deer run into the woods.

Brenda was talkative during the ride. She told him she was excited to be a mother and thanked him for supporting her.

He touched her hand and said, "I love you, Brenda. I would do anything for you." There was no reply from Brenda, and Tom felt sad for a moment.

Brenda continued talking about being a mother. She had so many wonderful ideas and plans.

Tom noted that Brenda mentioned only Dillon—she never once mentioned Donnie. He felt a terrible feeling brewing inside.

They arrived home to find a large box on the doorstep. Tom recognized the handwriting on the side as his sister's. Even as adults, Tracy was still looking out for him.

Tom left the box on the doorstep because they had to get the twins inside, settled and out of the cold.

Brenda unbuckled Dillon and went into the house. She did not return to help unpack the car.

When Tom brought Donnie into the house, Brenda was holding Dillon in the rocker and crying.

"Thanks a lot for your help, Brenda," he said.

"Sorry, honey. I just can't take my eyes off this angel from God," she replied.

"Don't forget you have two sons—not just one, Brenda." Tom could not shake the uneasy feeling, and it was getting the best of him.

Brenda silently rocked Dillon and stared at him like they were alone in the house.

It was as if Tom and Donnie were not in the room with them.

Tom fed Donnie a bottle and put him in his crib for a nap. He stood over his son and looked at him lovingly. *Brenda will certainly come to her senses and begin caring for Donnie as well as Dillon. How can she refuse such a darling child?*

Brenda was singing to Dillon in the living room.

He asked Brenda to stop singing since Donnie was down for a nap, but she ignored his request. She did not acknowledge his presence in any way.

"Brenda! Really! You are creeping me out! Snap the fuck out of whatever it is, and stop the damn singing! Please!"

She turned to him with a concerned look on her face. "I am sorry, Tom. I don't know what has come over me—but you don't have to take that tone with me!"

Tom walked over to her and got down on his knees. "Let's just forget about it, honey. I don't want to ruin this marvelous day."

She kissed his forehead. "Okay, Tom. My love, all is forgotten."

Remembering the box on the doorstep, Tom brought it inside and placed it on the kitchen table. He decided not to bother Brenda; he was already annoyed with her and felt it was best to leave her alone.

He grabbed a knife and opened the box. It was full of diapers, toys, clothes, and food for the whole family. There was a card at the bottom of the box: "Blessings and love to you all! What a wonderful addition to our happy family Donnie and Dillon will make. Much love, the Fam."

Tom always thought he had the best family in the world, and this clinched it.

Tom Sherrill was the youngest of ten children. Growing up on a working farm in a little town, he was raised to be a hard worker and a good person. He had become both and more.

The Sherrills celebrated all holidays and birthdays together. The children played long games of softball and volleyball in the hot sun, and the adults visited and prepared wonderful feasts. Tom couldn't wait to introduce their boys to his family. He thought about how he would spend year after year watching them running, playing, and laughing with their cousins. Tom had never felt such joy in his heart.

Tom heard crying coming from the nursery. It sounded like Donnie was awake. In the living room, Brenda was asleep in the rocker with Dillon on her chest. He stopped for a moment to look at the two of them lying there so peacefully. *What a precious sight to see mother and son.*

Donnie's cries grew stronger, and Tom hurried off to collect his son.

When Tom entered the nursery, he was filled with panic. A scarf was wrapped around Donnie's neck. He scooped up the child and freed him from the scarf. It was the scarf Brenda had worn that morning to the hospital. *How did it get into Donnie's crib? Brenda hadn't come anywhere near the nursery since they arrived home—or had she?*

Tom carried Donnie to the living room.

Brenda was still sleeping.

He bent down and whispered, "Brenda, wake up."

She jumped with a startle and said, "What the hell do you want, Tom? You woke me up out of a dead sleep."

He told her how he had found Donnie with her scarf wrapped around his neck.

She told him she didn't know how the scarf got there and got up from the rocker without acknowledging Donnie. She took Dillon into the master bedroom and closed the door behind her.

Tom sat down in the rocker with Donnie. *I can't believe what just happened.* He was in disbelief. She didn't kiss, hug, touch, or speak to her son. She acted like she didn't want anything to do with Donnie. In fact, she seemed angry. Tom began to cry.

Donnie put his tiny hand on Tom's face as if to say everything was okay.

The two drifted off to sleep.

Two hours later, Tom awoke to sounds coming from the nursery. He put Donnie in the baby rocker by the couch and ran into the nursery.

Brenda was dragging Dillon's crib to the door.

Tom shouted, "What are you doing now?"

She looked in his direction, startled. "Dillon is going to sleep in our bedroom now. He needs me."

Tom replied, "We did not discuss the twins sleeping in our room, Brenda. I do not think it is a good idea. We need our space, and they need theirs."

She looked at Tom with the same strange, spaced-out expression and said, "I said Dillon—not Donnie."

From the living room, Donnie cried out.

Tom ran to the living room and picked up the baby. He wondered if his son could feel that his mother wanted nothing to do with him. The little angel buried his head in Tom's shoulder and sobbed. He was the sweetest, most precious baby.

Tom was confused and scared. He didn't know what to do about Brenda and her favoritism of Dillon. Deep in his gut, he was certain Brenda had put the scarf around Donnie's neck or at least placed the scarf in his crib. Should he pursue this further with Brenda? Call the minister? Tom decided to sleep on it and find a solution in the morning.

With Brenda locked in the master bedroom with Dillon, he would stay on the sofa in the nursery. He did not have a good feeling about leaving the helpless child alone in his crib. He couldn't take any chances with Brenda acting like a crazy person. He knew he needed to figure out what was happening to his wife.

Tom laid on the sofa and listened to the sweet sounds of Donnie as he slept. The sounds were soothing and almost hypnotic. He was filled with so much love for his boys, but at the same time, he was very sad. It seemed as though adopting the twins had caused some kind of breakdown in Brenda. She woke up as the woman he married and went to bed like a stranger. He wondered how he could turn this situation around. Would he ever trust her again with Donnie? How could he after finding her scarf wrapped around the child's neck? He closed his eyes and slept.

The sun shining through the window in the nursery woke Tom from his sleep. He was surprised Donnie did not wake the entire night. Was it possible he could sleep for a solid seven hours? He was sure the baby would wake him to eat or for a diaper change.

Tom got up from the sofa and walked, quickly, to Donnie's crib, tripping on a pillow from the living room couch. He didn't remember bringing the pillow in with him. *How did the pillow get in here?*

Looking into the crib, he was horrified to find that Donnie was blue. He wasn't breathing, and his skin was icy cold. Checking Donnie's pulse, Tom realized the infant was dead. He collapsed to the floor in heart-wrenching sobs and screamed for Brenda, but she did not answer. He ran to the master bedroom, but she was gone—and so was Dillon.

Brenda's car was gone from the driveway. Tom was shaking. His chest hurt, and his breathing was rapid. He felt like he was going to have a heart attack. He ran into the bathroom, turned on the cold water, and began to splash his face. "Oh my God! What is happening?"

Tom rushed to the telephone and dialed 911. He explained to the dispatcher how Donnie was blue, cold, and had no pulse.

The dispatcher instructed him to keep his hands off the infant and asked him to wait on the porch for the ambulance.

He was overcome with grief and fell to the floor in tears, "No, no, no ..."

After a few moments, Tom went outside to wait on the porch. He grabbed his cell phone off the coffee table on his way out the door. As he waited, his thoughts wandered to Brenda and Dillon. *Where could she have possibly taken him so early in the morning? It is odd she would leave without telling him she was going out. She never left the house without at least leaving a note.* Tom had not found anything that resembled a note of any kind. *Did she have something to do with Donnie's death?* He felt sick to his stomach and vomited.

Tom dialed Brenda's cell number and waited for her to pick up. The phone rang over and over, but she did not answer. He reached her voice mail and left a message, telling her to call him immediately.

Tom heard the sirens from the ambulance as it raced down the street. As the paramedics rushed up the porch steps, they asked Tom to show them to Donnie and to step back so they would have room to work.

The first paramedic checked the child's pulse, finding none. The baby was blue and had been gone for what appeared to be hours. Donnie was pronounced dead on the scene.

Tom was unable to control his weeping as one of the paramedics led him from the nursery and sat him down on the couch in the living room. He looked up, wiping the tears from his eyes, as a second paramedic walked past him carrying a papoose with Donnie strapped to it. A white sheet covered the infant.

Tom was faced with the reality that his child was really dead. He decided to follow the ambulance to the hospital. He would need a ride home, and with Brenda nowhere to be found, it was the only solution.

He pulled into the hospital parking lot and decided to try Brenda again before entering the hospital. There was still no answer. He left another message, but this time, he told her to come to the hospital as soon as possible. He said, "Something terrible has happened. I need you here right away."

At the reception desk, Tom explained that an ambulance had just brought in his dead infant son.

The volunteer offered Tom her condolences and led him to a private waiting room. "The doctor will be in to speak with you shortly. Again, I am so sorry for your loss."

Tom thanked the nice lady and sat down to wait for the doctor.

Dr. Moore entered the waiting room and shook Tom's hand. The doctor offered his condolences and asked Tom to be seated. The doctor reported that all signs indicated Donnie's death was caused by sudden infant death syndrome (SIDS). "There will be an autopsy performed in the morning to determine the exact cause of the child's death." Dr. Moore told Tom he would call him when the results of the autopsy came in. He instructed Tom that the funeral home could pick up Donnie's body for burial preparation once the results of the autopsy were reported.

Tom gave the doctor his cell phone number, shook his hand again, and headed home.

When Tom pulled up to the house, Brenda's car was in the driveway. He ran into the house and yelled, "Brenda! Brenda come quickly!"

She ran into the living room. "Stop that yelling, Tom! I just put Dillon down for a nap."

Tom said, "Shut the fuck up, Brenda! Where the hell have you been? Donnie is dead!"

Brenda's face turned pale, and she began to cry. "What happened, Tom? Why didn't you call me?"

He began to pace. His face was red, and his forehead was wet with perspiration. "I did, Brenda. I called and called, but you didn't answer. I left two messages for you. Where have you been?"

"Dillon had a restless night. At four o'clock, I decided to pack him up and take him to my parents." New Berry Falls was out in the sticks, an hour away, and there was no cell service. "What happened? Where is my baby?"

He replied, "Your baby is there." He pointed at Dillon.

"That is not fair, Tom." Brenda fell to the floor and sobbed.

"The doctor will call us tomorrow to report the exact cause of death. Once the autopsy is completed, we can instruct the funeral home to pick up Donnie's body so he can be prepared for the funeral."

Brenda looked up at Tom and held out her hand.

He glared at her for a moment and then stormed out of the house, slamming the door behind him.

Once inside his truck, Tom buckled his seat belt, started the engine, and sped off, throwing rocks and dirt from his tires.

He set out for his mom and dad's farm. He knew they would welcome him with open arms. His parents had always stood beside him, and he needed their comfort now more than ever. The drive would take him thirty minutes, which was enough time to gather himself. He didn't want his mother to see him so upset. She had been struggling with heart problems for a year, and he didn't want her to get upset, which would raise her blood pressure.

He couldn't wait to fall into his mother's arms and cry.

# LOVING PARENTS

Tom's grip on the steering wheel loosened a bit as he pulled onto the long, dirt driveway. What a marvelous childhood he had spent at the family farm with his eight brothers and one sister.

His parents were liked in their little town. Ruby and Bernard were active in their church and close to all of their children. They went almost everywhere as a family.

Tom had nothing but good memories of growing up in Jackson. The town was small, there was little crime, and the corner restaurant was buzzing every Friday and Saturday night with pretty girls and hot rods. Kaila's Place was where he had met Brenda. When he was a senior—and she was a junior—Jackson High's varsity football team was playing in the championship at the stadium near Jackson Square. Brenda was there with friends, watching New Berry Falls play for the state championship against Jackson. They met at the restaurant after Jackson clobbered NBF 31–0.

Brenda didn't care much—she never followed football anyway. Tom fell in love with her the moment he laid eyes on her, and she felt the same way. Over the years, they had been very happy together. Only in the past five months had their marriage started to deteriorate.

He had no words for what was happening with Brenda

and their relationship now, but he was certain his mother and father would help him find the answers he was so desperately searching for.

He stepped out of his truck and was greeted by his dad. Bernard had been gathering eggs from the chicken coop when he saw his son coming up the driveway. He met Tom halfway to the house and hugged him for a long time. "Tom, what is wrong? I can see something has you upset. You can tell your old man anything."

Tom saw his mother appear at the door, and he took off running toward her. "Mom, Donnie is dead! He is gone, and I don't know why!"

Ruby took her youngest son, her baby, into her arms as he wept uncontrollably. She began to cry and asked, "What happened, honey? You can tell Mama."

Tom took her hand and led her into the house.

Bernard followed behind them and closed the door.

All family discussions were held at the kitchen table.

Tom told them what had happened. He hesitated when he got to the part about Brenda and Dillon being missing from the house when he made the discovery. If he mentioned that Brenda and Dillon had been missing when he discovered Donnie, his mother and father would have suspected Brenda. Neither of his parents had cared much for her. Ruby said she thought there was a sneaky and deceitful air about Brenda, and Bernard thought she was a bit uppity.

Ruby said, "Where was Brenda when all this was happening?"

Tom replied, "Brenda claims she took Dillon to her parents' house after he was up most of the night. She said she hoped the ride there and back would calm him."

Ruby put her hand on Tom's and said, "You mean to tell me you were alone when you found your son dead? Damn that woman! She has never been there for you, Tom! Will you ever learn?"

Bernard stood up and said, "Ruby, knock it off! Now is not the time for your lectures about how wrong Tom was in marrying Brenda. We all know it was the childish mistake of a teenager, but please save it for another time." Bernard was always willing to put his feelings aside and be there for his son.

Tom had been crying and angry for many hours, and he was exhausted.

Ruby told Tom to go upstairs and lie down. She would wake him when supper was ready.

Tom walked toward the stairs of the old farmhouse. A few stairs into his climb, he turned toward his folks and said, "I will always love Brenda." He continued up the stairs to his bedroom and shut the door behind him.

Ruby looked at Bernard and said, "She has really gone and done it now, Bernard. The crazy bitch killed one of their sons."

"Now, now, Mama. Don't go around pointing those kinds of fingers at people. It could get you into trouble."

Tom slept for three hours before Ruby went to wake him. She opened the door to Tom's bedroom, stood in the doorway, and looked at Tom for a few moments. He was her baby; he was her favorite, but she would never tell a soul. She thought about all the evenings and mornings she had stood in that doorway and watched her son sleep. There were so many. He was such a smart, bright, happy child, and he had grown into the most amazing man. She was so proud of her little Tommy.

"Tom?" she called out.

"I'm up, Mom. Thanks. I will be right down."

She turned from his room and started down the stairs.

Bernard was greeting someone at the kitchen door as she entered the dining room. When she got to the kitchen, she heard Brenda's voice. She had come looking for her husband after all.

"Hello, Ruby," Brenda said.

"Good day to you," replied Ruby. "What are you doing here?" She hoped her son would not walk down the stairs until she had a chance to get rid of the snotty New Berry bitch. Ruby let out a giggle.

"Is Tom here?" Brenda asked.

Just as Ruby was about to unleash all hell on Brenda, Bernard raised his hand to silence her. He calmly said, "Why, yes, he is, dear. We are so sorry to hear about Donnie. What a shame. It is heartbreaking news to say the least. You must understand the horrific scene it was for Tom, especially being all alone in the house. Please, Brenda, out of respect for him and all the years you have been together, please leave him to us until he is ready to speak to you."

Brenda walked toward the dining room, but Ruby stepped between her and the doorway. "You heard Bernard—now go on and let us take care of *our* boy. We will let him know you were here."

Brenda's face turned bright red, and she looked like she would explode into tears of rage.

Ruby said, "By the way Brenda, where is our other grandson?"

Brenda knew not to pick a fight with her mother-in-law. Ruby outweighed her by at least twenty-five pounds and was a good five inches taller than the young, fresh-faced mother.

"He is with the neighbor, Ruby. He is fine. I did not think it would be safe to take him out on these roads. The weatherman said we got at least five inches of snow on the ground—and more is on the way. You should really mind your own business, Mom."

Ruby simply walked to the door and opened it. As Brenda walked past her, Ruby felt a cold chill pass through her body. She could not deny the overpowering feeling of evil she experienced at that very moment. She knew there would be more trouble to come.

Fifteen minutes later, Tom walked into the kitchen.

Bernard said, "Good grief, son. What took you so long? Some things never change."

"I heard Brenda's voice and thought it would be a good idea to stay upstairs. When she did not leave right away, I decided to take a shower. I hope that is okay. It really helped. I feel a little better."

Ruby kissed her son on the cheek and said, "This will always be your home, Tom. You treat it as such, you hear?"

Tom hugged her and said, "Okay, Mama. What did Brenda say?"

Bernard looked at his son and grinned. "Not much, son. You know your mother is like a mama lion—ain't nobody gonna harm her cub. We asked her to leave you alone until you can wrap your head around what happened."

Tom let out a sigh of relief, and the tension from his shoulders let up a little. "Thanks, Mom. I knew I could count on you both."

They ate their tuna sandwiches and homemade vegetable soup in silence.

After supper, Tom went back up to his bedroom to check his cell phone for messages. There was only one, and it was from Brenda. She had left the message before she showed up at the farm. She sounded like she was out of her mind with grief and sadness. He thought about jumping in his truck and heading home. *No, I can't go home—not right now.* The resentment and anger he felt toward her needed to be dealt with before he could speak to her. In his heart, he loved her, but deep down in his stomach, he knew she had killed their son. He would wait and contact her after the doctor called with the autopsy results.

Tom heard his dad calling his name from downstairs. He put his phone on its charger and headed downstairs to see what he wanted.

Bernard was sitting at the dining room table with a jug of moonshine and two beers. "Sit down, son, and have a drink with your pops."

Tom took a seat across the table from his dad.

"How are you doing, son? Is there anything I can do for you? Tell me ... please. How can I help you, my dear boy?"

Tom looked up from his beer. "You are already helping me, Dad. Just being here with you and Mom means the world to me. I can always trust you guys to have my back."

Pouring a shot for his son, Bernard said, "Why don't you let your mom and I take care of the funeral arrangements after you hear from the doctor tomorrow? You have enough on your plate. Let us do this for you."

Tom drank down the shot, chasing it with a swig of his beer. "Thanks, Dad. I would appreciate it very much. I figured you and Mom would suggest calling Mr. Graves."

Barton Graves was the only mortician in Jackson. He was one of his parents' oldest and dearest friends. As a child, Tom was afraid of Mr. Graves. He was pale, thin, and creepy. The funeral home was big and dark. It was a hundred-year-old house on a horse ranch that reminded Tom of the house from *Psycho*. As a kid, he had run past the spooky place every day on his way to and from school.

"Okay then. Your mother will call him tomorrow and make all the arrangements." Bernard excused himself and said he was turning in for the night.

Tom watched as his dad walked from the room. He could hear his mother washing the supper dishes. The sounds of the house soothed him, and he poured another shot.

Ruby came into the dining room and said, "Go ahead and pour me one of those while you are at it, honey." She sat down next to Tom, downed her shot, and patted her son on the back. "When you are ready to talk about what happened and what you are feeling, let me know. You can talk to me about anything. You will always be my baby. I love you."

Tom thanked his mom and told her he would be fine.

She said good night and went upstairs.

He sat for a moment, reflecting on the day's events with tears in his eyes. He hoped it was all a dream he would soon wake up from. He turned off the lights and headed off to bed.

Tom woke to the smell of bacon and coffee at six the next morning. For a moment, he forgot where he was and what had happened the day before. As he got out of his bed and looked around, the memories came flooding back to him. *Poor Donnie*, he thought.

He decided to maintain his composure today—no matter what the coroner reported. His parents were already upset enough; he didn't want to make matters worse. With the spitfire he had for a mother, who knows what she might do.

He put on his robe and headed downstairs for a cup of coffee.

Ruby smiled and said, "You still take your coffee with cream and sugar, right?"

Tom nodded and sat down at the table as she handed him a cup of coffee. He glanced at his cell phone. Brenda had not called, which was a bit odd. He decided to give her a call. "I will be right back, Mom. I think I should call the house to be sure everything is all right with Brenda and Dillon. I would never forgive myself if something happened to them and I was nowhere around. 'Two wrongs don't make a right.'"

Ruby said, "Yeah, Tom. You don't want to leave her alone like she did to you and your son."

Tom walked out to the porch to talk in private. He knew his mom was right; it seemed she had been all along. Her remark was a reminder to Tom to stay strong and not give in to Brenda like he always did. He was determined to help Brenda—but on his terms and not hers.

Brenda picked up her phone on the second ring. "Tom, are you okay? You still at the farm? Has the doctor called?"

Dillon was cooing in the background.

"No. I was calling to check on you and the baby to make sure you are both okay. I will be home by dark tonight. I will call you as soon as I hear from the doctor."

"So, you will be home for good tonight, Tom? You will not be going back to stay at the farm?"

He was glad to hear the hope in her voice, but he thought it was strange that she didn't sound more upset over the death of her son. She was more concerned with Tom coming home than the fact that they would be burying their son in the next few days. "Yes. I will be home to stay, but we need to sit down and talk through our issues, Brenda. We can call the minister, see a therapist, whatever we decide as a couple. You and I decide together as a team. Okay?"

"Okay, Tom. I will talk to you later then. Love you."

Tom hesitated for a moment before he said, "I love you too, Brenda."

The day seemed to drag on and on. Finally, at one thirty, Tom's cell phone rang. His pulse quickened as he answered the call. "Hello? This is Tom."

"Hi, Tom. I am Dr. Bauer. I performed the autopsy on your son's body. First, I want to convey my sincere condolences for your loss. We are all so very sorry … our deepest sympathies to your family. With your permission, I am ready to tell you what my findings were. May I continue?"

Tom was ready to get it over with so he could lay his son to rest and begin the much-needed mourning process. "Please continue, Dr. Bauer."

"Thank you, Tom. I have concluded your son's death was caused by sudden infant death syndrome. When I looked at the report, I read that you stated you put Donnie on his back when you put him to sleep the night before, correct?"

Tom was crying as he replied, "Yes, Dr. Bauer. I put my son to bed on his back, and seven hours later, I found him dead on his back. He had not turned over … it didn't look like he had moved at all. I thought SIDS killed babies who slept on their stomachs. Is that correct?"

When they found out Brenda was pregnant, they both began reading all the parenting magazines and books they could get their hands on. After the pregnancy was lost, he continued reading the material in the hopes that the information would come in handy someday. Somehow, the reading soothed him.

The doctor said, "Yes, Tom. In nearly all cases of SIDS, the infants are found to have been sleeping on their stomachs, but there are cases every year in which children have been found on their backs. Are there any other questions I can answer for you?"

Tom grabbed a tissue from his pocket and said, "No. Thank you, Doctor. I have no more questions. I appreciate you taking time to call me. May we tell Mr. Graves that he can collect our son's body so he can be prepared for burial?"

"Yes, Tom. He is all set to be transferred. Again, my condolences on the loss of your child. God be with you."

When Tom walked into the kitchen, his mother was preparing one of Tom's favorite meals: barbequed chicken, corn on the cob, homemade biscuits, and apple pie.

Ruby looked up from kneading the dough and asked, "That the doctor? What did he say?"

He walked toward her and said, "The cause of death was SIDS. The doctor said it is not as common for babies to die on their backs, but it does happen."

Ruby put her arms around her son and hugged him. "I am so sorry for your loss, honey. If there was anything I could do to take your pain away, I would." She left the kitchen to call Barton Graves to arrange for the transport of her grandson's body to the funeral home.

Tom sat down at the kitchen table and picked up his cell phone to call Brenda. The phone went immediately to voicemail. He wondered why she would turn off her phone when she knew he was supposed to call her after he spoke with the doctor.

He decided to leave her a message with the autopsy results. After all, she already knew Dr. Moore told him that he believed Donnie had died from SIDS. The news shouldn't come as a shock to her. Tom said, "Brenda, I got a call from the doctor. The cause of death was SIDS ... just as Dr. Moore said previously. My parents are making the funeral arrangements. We need to focus on each other and Dillon. I will see you tonight."

In the kitchen, Ruby was shucking the corn in a large soup pot. She looked at him with loving, kind eyes and said, "Barton is on his way over to the hospital now. There will be a showing from four until eight on Friday and one on Saturday from ten until noon. There will be a short service performed by Reverend Holt following the Saturday showing. I have instructed Barton to cremate Donnie's body. Did I miss anything? I will take care of flowers and the obituary too."

Tom rubbed his mom's back for a moment and said, "Thank you so much for all of your help, Mom. I am so lucky to have you and Dad. I might as well tell you now … After dinner I am going home. I need to be with Brenda and Dillon. I promise I will keep my eyes and ears open, Mom. And when I am ready, there are some things I need to tell you about all of this. Right now, I just cannot bring myself to talk about any of it. I know you understand. I love you, Mom!"

Ruby turned to her son and kissed him on the cheek. "I love you too, Tommy. I always have and always will! Even when my time on earth is done, I will live on in your heart. I am part of you, and you are a part of me. Your father and I are with you wherever you go. As you raise Dillon, you will grow to understand why parents say and do what we do for our children. Son, I would die for you."

"You are the best mom a son could ask for," Tom said as he hugged her.

"Now go on outside and get your dad. Supper is ready." Ruby walked over to the refrigerator and took out the butter for the corn.

Tom got his dad, and they washed their hands before dinner.

Once seated, Bernard said, "Dear Lord, thank you for this food we are about to eat. We ask for your guidance now and always. We thank you for taking Donnie—son, grandson, and brother—into your kingdom. Please help see our family through this terrible tragedy. We love you, Lord. Amen."

"Amen." Ruby, Tom, and Bernard raised their heads.

Supper was wonderful as usual. Ruby was a tough, beautiful woman, and she was one hell of a good cook. Bernard loved to tease her by saying the only reason he married her was because she was such a marvelous cook. Tom knew it was a joke since Bernard loved Ruby with every fiber in his body. She was his world.

They talked about the new greenhouse Ruby and Bernard had purchased. Bernard had recruited Tom to help him with the construction. They decided to start working on it as soon as possible. Bernard was hoping winter would slow enough for them to get to work on it soon. Tom looked forward to assisting in all his dad's projects. He was a lot of fun to work with, and there was never a dull moment. Bernard was handy, and ever since he could remember, Tom thought his dad could do anything.

Ruby got up from the table and said, "Well, I better cut this pie so you can get on the road before it gets dark, son. The snow is starting to come down again, and you don't want to get stuck in a blizzard."

He thanked his mom for thinking of his safety and agreed that they should get to dessert. "Another masterpiece, Mother," Tom said as he inhaled the last bite of apple pie. He got up from the table, rinsed off his plate and coffee mug, kissed Ruby, shook Bernard's strong, callused hand, and headed toward the door.

Ruby said, "Make sure you call us when you pull into your driveway!"

"Okay, Mama," he said as he walked outside.

# GOING HOME

Tom felt the bad feeling creeping back into him as he got closer to home. He did not know what he might find when he got there. He thought about the scarf around Donnie's neck and was having a hard time accepting that one of his sons was dead. For goodness' sake, the twins had not even been part of the family for a full twenty-four hours when Donnie died. He felt like turning his truck around and running back to the farm. He wanted to speed back to his mom and dad's house. He always felt safe there. *No, I have to go home and face this head-on. I have to deal with whatever is ahead of me. I have to talk to Brenda. I can't put if off any longer.*

As Tom pulled into the driveway, he looked at his watch. The trip had taken longer than usual. The snow had been coming down so heavy that he was only able to see about three feet in front of him. It usually took thirty minutes each way, but it had taken an hour and a half to get home from the farm.

Before he got out of his car, he picked up his cell phone and saw that his mother had already called him twice. Tom dialed, and Ruby picked up on the first ring. She must have been waiting for his call. "Hi, Mom. I made it. It was slow going with the snow so heavy. I could only see a few feet in front of me. I am sorry I worried you and Dad."

Ruby said, "Oh, thank God! I was pacing the floor, waiting for your call. Your father said it would take longer to get home, but you know me, I am such a worrywart. Thank you so much for calling us, Tom. Good luck with Brenda. Please call me in the morning—or sooner if you need to. We love you, son."

He smiled and said, "I love you both very much, and I will call you in the morning. Sweet dreams. Good night." Tom hung up the phone, got out of the truck, and walked toward the house.

Before he reached the door, Brenda opened it and ran to him with open arms. "Oh, Tom. It is so good to have you home. I missed you. I am so sorry I wasn't there for you. Please forgive me."

He put down his backpack and took Brenda into his arms. "I forgive you, Brenda, and I love you very much."

Walking into the house, Tom did not see anything out of the ordinary. The house was neat and tidy like it normally was, and nothing seemed to be out of place. Dillon was in the playpen by the couch, staring at the ceiling fan that was turning above his head. The baby was fixated on the fan and never took his eyes off of it. Tom watched his son for several minutes. There was something strange about the way Dillon was looking at the fan. The child's face had a sinister glow to it.

"Downright weird," Tom said.

"What did you say, honey? I could not hear you," Brenda called out from the kitchen.

"I said I am glad I'm here," Tom lied.

*There is something so strange about the way he is looking at the fan,* he thought.

Tom was not going to mention anything to Brenda about his suspicions. If she did have something to do with his son's death, he would find out by waiting and watching. There was just no mistaking the changes in Brenda and her disappearance with Dillon. Tom was not a man who believed in coincidence.

He walked away from the playpen without picking up Dillon. The baby was entertained and happy, and Tom decided to have his talk with Brenda while he had the chance. He walked into the kitchen and asked Brenda to sit with him at the table.

She said, "Do you want some coffee?"

Tom sat down and said, "Yes, please. That would be great."

She brought over two cups of coffee and handed Tom one that said: "World's Greatest Dad." Brenda's said: "World's Greatest Mom." He had not seen the coffee mugs before, and he liked them very much. "Where did you get these, Bren?" Tom held up his mug.

"I picked them up at the Mobil gas station on the corner of Route 480, right before the New Berry Falls city limits. I got them on my way back from my mom and dad's earlier this week."

*Oh, yeah. That's right ... the day your son died,* Tom thought. Thoughts of his mother popped into his head. He obviously got his sarcasm from her. It was a reminder to him that he must be strong and stand his ground with Brenda. "Okay, I am not going to harp, lecture, or nag, Brenda. We have been through this before—many times. You know how I feel about marriage or any relationship for that matter. You have gotten back into your controlling ways. You left and drove our son an hour away without even a note. You haven't done that in years. And then you moved Dillon into our bedroom without discussing it with me first. I refuse to live with *that* Brenda ever again. If you want to have Dillon's crib in the bedroom with you, that is fine. When we were reading all the baby books, I read about the many insecurities of new parents, especially mothers, and I realize it will be less stressful for you if Dillon sleeps in the master bedroom. However, I will not be able to sleep in the same room with him. I sleep very lightly and would never be able to sleep with him waking up for bottles, changing diapers, and crying. I have to be able to sleep so I can go to work each day and be alert. If it is okay with you, I think we should sleep separately for now. You can wake me up anytime you want me to tend to the baby or if you need help with anything. I want to do my share. What do you think, Bren?"

She got up from her chair and poured herself another cup of coffee. "I promise to work on suppressing my controlling tendencies, Tom. I am so sorry I have upset and neglected you. I did not intend to. I am fine with sleeping separately. Thank you for understanding my feelings. I am very glad to have you home."

Tom got up and massaged her shoulders. "Okay. I will start moving my things into the spare bedroom tonight." He kissed the top of her head and went to the master bedroom to collect his belongings.

Brenda went into the living room to check on Dillon. He was still staring at the ceiling fan. She had settled into the role of mother very quickly. She looked down at Dillon and said, "My son, my lovely, only beautiful son. I love you more than anything. I would die for you."

Tom came into the living room and said, "Did you get my email with the showings and service times for Donnie?"

She jumped a little and said, "Yes, dear. I got it just after you sent it."

He looked at her and said, "Okay. You didn't mention receiving the times for your dead son's funeral—so I thought you might not have gotten it. We need to be at the funeral home by three o'clock on Friday afternoon. I will take an outfit to Barton Graves tomorrow. Do you want to come?"

She cocked her head and snarled. "The funeral is in Jackson? Why in the hell would your fucking parents have the funeral in Jackson?"

Tom said, "Why would you think otherwise, Brenda? Dr. Graves is a dear, old friend of our family. When you were okay with Mom and Dad planning the funeral, I assumed you would already understand that. I am sorry I was not more specific. I am going to excuse myself for the evening. Good night." He picked up Dillon, held him to his chest, and rocked from side. He whispered, "I love you," placed him in the playpen, and went to the master bedroom to pick out an outfit for Donnie.

He had to take the outfit to Barton Graves in the morning. "Poor little guy," Tom said. Tears began to flow as he looked through the tiny clothes. He selected one of the outfits his parents had given them. It was designed to look like a tuxedo and would be perfect for the showing.

Tom went to the spare room and closed the door behind him. He sat down on the bed with a sigh of relief. He could not stop thinking about the look of rage on Brenda's face when she commented about the funeral being held in Jackson. Everything about what had happened scared the hell out of him. He was relieved to be sleeping in the spare room. At least he would have a place to escape if he needed to. He put some of his clothes in the small dresser and hung the rest up in the closet. He set his alarm for five o'clock, turned off the light, said his prayers, and drifted off to sleep.

When Tom's alarm sounded, he got right out of bed. He

did not hit the snooze button over and over like he normally did. He called his mother and left a message to let her know he was heading to the farm with the outfit for Donnie. They would all go to the funeral home to see Barton Graves. He told her she could expect him around seven o'clock, and there was no need to call him back. If she called him back, she would keep him on the phone forever and delay his departure. Tom hung up and headed downstairs.

After starting the coffee, he went back upstairs to take his shower. He was hoping to leave before Brenda woke up. After her little fit, he was not in the mood for any aftershocks. The next few days were not about her—they were about their dead son.

He showered, got dressed, grabbed his duffel bag, and headed downstairs to get some coffee. He could hear Brenda talking to Dillon as he approached the nursery.

She said, "You are the best boy in the whole, wide world, my sweet angel. We didn't need that other baby, did we? Just us—isn't that right, precious? Mommy told you she would make him go away, didn't she?"

Tom felt like he had been kicked in the chest. *Oh my God!* He hurried downstairs and decided to stop for coffee on his way to the farm. Right then, all he wanted was to get out of that house.

He pulled into the Dairy Mart on the corner of Broad and Naples Streets. He was in desperate need of coffee. He had half a tank of gas, and he would have to stop in Jackson if he did not fuel up in Canyon Heights. Fuel was more expensive in Canyon Heights.

As he walked into the store to grab some coffee and pay for his gas, Detective Shae Tomkins came up to Tom. The officer was in charge of the homicide department at the Canyon Heights Police Department.

The Canyon Heights PD had an annual pancake breakfast in one of Old Man Peterson's barns, about a quarter mile from Tom and Brenda's place. It was the old fella's annual contribution to the police department. The couple had walked to the pancake breakfast for the past three years. "Hey, Tom. I hope you and Brenda are hanging in there. We are all so sorry to hear about the loss of your son. If there is anything any of us at the CHPD can do for you, please let me or one of the other officers know. You know where to find us."

Tom shook Shae's hand and said, "Thank you very much, Detective Tomkins, I will pass on your condolences to Brenda." He continued into the store, bought his coffee, and paid for his fuel. As he walked past the candy aisle, he noticed a display case of coffee and cups. Two of the mugs caught his eye: "World's Greatest Dad" and "World's Greatest Mom." Tom stared at the display case for a few moments. *What are the chances two different businesses would carry these mugs?* He was sure he had caught Brenda in a lie.

As he headed down the road, Tom flipped through the radio stations. His CD player was broken, and he had to make do with the radio. He heard a familiar voice and smiled. His favorite musician of all time—Elvis Presley—was singing "You're the Devil in Disguise." Tom laughed to himself and thought it was ironic and rather fitting after the past couple of days. He turned up the radio and put his foot down on the accelerator.

He arrived at the farm at 7:05, and Ruby was standing at the door. Since he was five minutes late, she was probably freaking out in case Brenda had killed him too.

He grabbed the duffel bag and got out of his truck.

Ruby opened the door for her son and kissed him on the cheek.

He hugged her and said, "Good morning, Mama. I've got Donnie's outfit in this bag. I am gonna let you be in charge of giving it to Barton if you don't mind. I will put it by your purse."

She followed him into the kitchen.

He put down the bag and poured himself a cup of coffee.

Bernard sat at the end of the large table. "Come on, son. Sit and have some breakfast. I am sure you haven't eaten yet."

When he was a kid, Tom used to color and do his homework at the very same table. He sat next to his dad.

Ruby sat down across from Tom and said, "How did things go last night, baby?"

Bernard looked up from his paper.

Tom ran his fingers through his jet-black hair. "Not as good as I had hoped. I had a short and to-the-point talk with Brenda. We decided that she and Dillon would sleep together in the master bedroom—and I get the spare bedroom. I made the mistake of asking if she had received the email I sent about the showing and service times for the baby. She got shitty over the fact that the funeral is in Jackson. She had the most deranged look on her face. She was shaking, and drool came from her mouth as she yelled at me. She is not right in the head, and after you hear what I have to say, you will be convinced—as I am—that Brenda killed Donnie and has lost her mind." Tom told them about the scarf, the pillow, and how she hadn't seemed the least bit interested in Donnie—even at the hospital. Tom also told his folks about Brenda's eerie and incriminating words that morning.

Ruby stood up and slammed her fists on the table. "You

have to contact the police, Tom! We cannot allow her to get away with this. I knew she was trouble the first time I looked into her eyes. That fucking bitch!"

Bernard got up from the table, stood behind Tom, and put his hands on his son's shoulders. "We are so sorry you are going through this, son, but you are going to have to tell someone. She has taken a life and should pay for it. Brenda must be punished."

Tom got up and poured himself another cup of coffee. When he turned around, he was crying. His whole life was turned upside down—and Brenda was the cause of it. "You two are right. I need to tell someone, and I did. I told you guys. If I go to the police, they will want evidence, which I do not have. I didn't see Brenda put the scarf around Donnie's neck. I did not see her kill him, and I didn't record what she said to Dillon. The police will say it is my word against hers. If I go to the police right now, it will solve nothing—and Brenda will know we are on to her. The best way to catch her is to watch and wait for something solid we can use against her. Do you understand what I am saying?"

His parents nodded.

Ruby said, "I had not thought about it that way, Tom. I am sorry for getting so upset, but you are our son—and we will always protect and fight for you."

He had only heard his mother apologize a few times. "Thanks, Mom. I knew you both would understand once you were calm." Tom hugged his mother and grabbed three more strips of bacon.

Bernard let out a yawn and said, "Well, family, let's finish up breakfast and go see Barton. When we get back, will you have some time to hang out with your old man before you head back to Canyon Heights?"

Tom looked at his dad for a moment and said, "I always have time for you, Pops! What do you have in mind?"

Bernard got up from the table and put his plate and coffee mug in the sink. "I want to run a few ideas past you about the greenhouse. It was delivered yesterday, and it is as big as a Mack truck! I want you to help me lay out the lines so I can start digging out for the foundation next weekend. It will help me take all this shit off my mind for a bit. That okay with you?"

Tom put his dirty dishes in the sink and said, "Sure, Dad. I will help in any way I can. I hope you got that old backhoe working because you ain't gonna want to dig that by hand."

Ruby threw her head back and laughed loudly. "You didn't see the new toy your silly old dad bought himself, did you?"

Tom looked out the window and saw a brand-new Case CX17B, which was, in Tom's opinion, the best compact excavator money could buy. "Wow, Dad! You have really outdone yourself this time. I get to drive it, right?"

Bernard started to laugh. "We'll see, son. I know how you drive that truck, and I don't want you to wreck my baby."

Ruby stood up and walked toward the living room. "All right, you two. Have your pissing contest later. We need to get to Barton's. We are already late."

When they arrived at the funeral home, Barton was waiting in the lounge with a cup in his hand.

"I bet there is more than coffee in that mug, Mr. Graves," Bernard shouted as soon as he saw his old pal. There was no telling how many jugs of moonshine those two had retired over the years.

Barton got up and said, "You sure got me pegged, ya old bastard! How the hell are you?"

The two men embraced, slapping each other on the back as they did so.

"You are a lovely woman, Ruby," Mr. Graves said as he kissed her left hand.

Ruby's face flushed, and she said, "Oh, hush, ya old slut. Gimme a hug!" She had grown up with Barton chasing after her, and she had almost let him catch her until Bernard did. "Sure dodged that bullet," Ruby said under her breath. Barton had not gotten better-looking with age, and it looked as if he had gained at least sixty pounds.

Barton turned to Tom and said, "How are you, son? I was so sorry to hear of your loss. I will take care of everything. I am honored to do so and with no cost to any of you. I am happy to be able to do it for people I have loved my entire life. I can still remember watching you run past this funeral home on your way to school. I can see it plain as the nose on my face. I laughed and often thought of yelling 'Boo,' but I thought I might give you a heart attack or stroke."

Tom was slightly embarrassed and said, "I never thought you knew how creepy this place was." He took a Styrofoam cup from the stack and filled it with water.

Barton giggled "What do you mean was, Tom? This place is, was, and always will be creepy!"

They all laughed together as Barton led them into his office.

Ruby said, "Here is an outfit for our grandson."

"Thanks, dear. I will take care of it. There is just the matter of picking out the urn." He handed her some photos. "I have all of these in stock. Take these pictures home, Ruby, and call me later with what you all decide. Okay?"

She thanked him and kissed him on the cheek.

Bernard said, "If that is all there is, why don't we all go have lunch?"

They all agreed and walked out toward Bernard's truck.

In Jackson, there was only one place to have a meal if the Sherrill family was eating out: Kaila's Place.

Bernard pulled the truck into the last parking space in the lot. Walking around to the passenger door, he opened it, took Ruby's hand, and helped her step down from the truck. Tom watched his dad and thought about how he had never seen his mother get out of any vehicle without his father opening the door for her. *Amazing how such a hard-ass could be so romantic and sweet,* he thought.

The restaurant was packed, but they all knew there would be no problem getting a seat.

Barton and Kaila were cousins, and they had grown up playing together down at Blackgore Creek.

Kaila looked up from behind the cash register, grabbed four menus, and said, "Oh my. It is so wonderful to see you all! Please come with me." She led them to a large, empty room that had a chain across the doorway.

Tom had spent many birthdays and holidays in the banquet room. It was also where his parents had hosted his wedding reception.

"No family or friend of mine is going to put their name on a waiting list at my place," Kaila said as she put the menus on the table. "I know there ain't a one of ya that needs a menu, but just in case one of you old-timers have forgotten the menu items, here ya go." She laughed and walked back to the register.

Kaila came back to the table ten minutes later and took a seat next to Barton. "I am going to take an early lunch today. Can't pass up the chance to dine with my favorite people."

Kaila's granddaughter Maggie walked in and took their orders. Everyone at the table ordered the Jackson burger cooked medium.

The Jackson was the best burger Tom had ever eaten, and it was the only thing he ever ordered at Kaila's Place. He couldn't remember having a better lunch at Kaila's. Maybe it was all the good company and wonderful conversation. He felt sad that he was enjoying himself so much with his son's death being the reason he was even in the restaurant, but he was happy to have the distraction. His thoughts drifted to Brenda and how much he wished she was there with him. At least he wished the "old Brenda" was there.

Kaila picked up the check as always and told Ruby she would see everybody at the showing the following afternoon. She also said she would be very happy to prepare the food for the memorial lunch on Saturday.

Ruby said, "I would expect nothing less, Kaila. Go ahead with the usual deli, cheese, and bread plates. Please make up a few pastry boxes too. I am thinking at least a hundred people. We will be paying for your service, Kaila, and I will not take any guff from you about it? Okay?"

Kaila grunted and said, "God forbid I argue with you. I will take care of transporting, setting up everything, and serving with absolutely no fee to you. Deal?"

Ruby hugged her old friend and said, "Deal."

The trio dropped Barton off at the funeral home and steered the truck toward the farm. The snow was coming down hard, and Bernard was nervous driving in the whiteouts.

Ruby said, "Daddy do you want me to drive? You are no good in this kind of weather." He pulled the truck over and let Ruby drive. She slid into the driver's seat and took off down the road.

Arriving safely home, Bernard let out a sigh and said, "Whew—that was close, woman. You drive like a maniac. I was in fear for my life on that bumpy ride home."

Ruby laughed and shook her head. "Okay, old man. You don't want to get this started." She took his hand and led him into the house.

Tom followed them. "Dad, I don't think we will be snapping any lines today for the greenhouse foundation." A drift of snow covered at least five feet of the boom on the brand-new excavator. "You need to move that machine into one of those big-ass barns you have in the back, Pops. The hydraulics are going to freeze. I can't believe you left it out there. You would be chewing a hole in my ass the size of Louisville if I had left it out in the snow like that. Which one can I park it in? I am going to go out and shovel it off and then move it for you."

Bernard scratched his head and said, "Go ahead and put it in the far-left barn. There ain't one thing in it, and I swept it clean last week. Let me get my warm boots on, and I will go out with you."

Tom pulled the excavator into the barn and jumped off. "Nice ride, Dad! We are going to have some fun with this baby!"

Bernard gave his son a pat on the back and said, "Indeed we are, son! As soon as this damn snow quits, we can get to work on digging out for the foundation. Gonna let you do the digging, big guy."

The two stared at the snow outside the barn. It was coming down in sheets.

"Well, you better get on the road soon. Looks like it is fixing to turn nasty. Your mom will wear a hole in the carpet, pacing, until she hears you have made it home safely."

Tom laughed, "Yeah. You're right, Dad. Let's get in the house. I will have a cup of coffee with you guys and then take off."

Tom could smell Ruby's coffee when they walked in the door.

"Sit down, boys, and get warm." She walked over to the table with two cups.

Tom drank his, pushed his chair away from the table, and kissed his mom on the nose. "See you tomorrow, Mama. I will call you when I get home."

She smiled and said, "You be sure to do that, son. Be careful love."

Bernard walked his son to the door. "Love you, boy. Be safe. Hang in there. We will get through this together—like we always do."

"Thanks, Dad. I love you too. I will be here at two thirty tomorrow. Do your best to stay out of Brenda's way tomorrow, okay?"

Bernard shook his son's hand and said, "We can only promise that we will do our best, son. Now get going."

Tom got into his truck and started for Canyon Heights.

He pulled into the driveway and called his parents to let them know he was home.

Ruby said, "Hello, honey. You made it home okay? We love you so much. See you tomorrow afternoon."

Tom said, "Okay, Mama. Love to you and Pops! See you then." He hung up the phone and went inside. The house smelled like chocolate chip cookies—Tom's favorite. He could sniff them out from yards away. He put down the duffel bag with Donnie's outfit and walked into the kitchen.

Dillon was sleeping in his bassinet, and Brenda was baking cookies.

"Somebody is in a good mood," he said as he hugged his wife.

"Well, not so much a good mood with all that has

happened. Let's just say I am in a humble mood. A peace offering?" Brenda held up a cookie for Tom.

"Well, since you put it that way, Bren!" He smiled as he took the cookie from her manicured hand. *When did she find time to go to the nail salon? Who gets a manicure before a funeral?* He thought it best to leave it alone for now. It was just another nail in her coffin as far as he was concerned.

"Dinner will be ready in about twenty minutes, dear. If you want to take a shower before we eat, you have plenty of time."

*She is acting like nothing is wrong—as if we aren't burying our son tomorrow.*

"Thanks, hon. I think I will do that," Tom said as he walked up the stairs to the bathroom.

The shower felt good, and it relaxed him. He dried off, got dressed, combed his hair, and went downstairs.

Brenda was serving supper when he walked into the kitchen. "Perfect timing," she said.

Another one of Tom's favorite meals was T-bone steaks, baked potato, peas, and spinach salad. "Smells good, Bren. You have out done yourself. How is Dillon?" He looked at the sleeping baby and wondered if he missed his brother.

"He is a perfect angel. I don't think any of this will have any effect on him. He is certainly too young to know what has happened."

"I don't know about that," Tom said. "I read a book that had a whole chapter dedicated to twins. One of the doctors conducted a study for three months. During the first part of the study, five sets of twins went through their everyday life side by side. They ate, slept, bathed, and were changed simultaneously. During the second part of the study, the twins were separated and did not see each other for a month.

The babies cried more than normal, refused to eat, and had trouble sleeping through the night."

Brenda looked over at the sleeping baby. "Well, you can relax, Tom. He is fine. You leave my boy to me. I know what he needs."

He looked down at his plate for the remainder of supper. He couldn't stand to look across the table at his wife. "All finished. It was good, Bren." Tom got up from the table, washed off his plate, and said, "Tomorrow is going to be a long day. I am going to turn in early. Good night, Brenda." He bent down and kissed Dillon as he walked by. "'Night, son." Tom went upstairs and closed the door, locking it behind him.

Tom awoke the next morning to the sound of Brenda singing to Dillon. Looking at the clock, he saw that it was already ten. "Damn it. My alarm didn't go off." He rushed out of bed.

The singing in the master bedroom was not pleasant or sweet. The sound of her voice, when she sang to Dillon, sickened him. He was growing tired of pretending that Brenda wasn't crazy. He was filled with hatred for her and wanted to be free of her, but he had to have solid evidence to prove that she had killed their son. Once he had something concrete, he would take it to Detective Shae Tomkins. Until then, he had to wait and watch.

After turning on the shower, Tom paused and went back into the bedroom. He popped his favorite CD in the stereo and turned the volume higher. "There," Tom said. "No more Brenda."

He was finishing up his coffee when his wife came downstairs. "Good," he said. "You're up. I am going to Old Man Peterson's place for a little bit. We got a lot of snow overnight, and that old man will have a heart attack out there shoveling. He won't use that new snowblower his sister bought for him. I am going to take our tractor down there and dig him out. We need to get on the road no later than one o'clock this afternoon. Donnie's showing starts at four, and Barton wants us there by three. It will most likely take at least an hour to get to Mom and Dad's with this nasty weather."

She put Dillon in his rocker, walked up to Tom, and kissed him full on the mouth. "No problem, honey. My boy and I will be ready to go."

# 4 PETERSEN

Adam Peterson owned 150 acres of land that surrounded Tom and Brenda's place. The land had been in his family for more than a century. Tom figured Peterson, as he liked to be called, had to be in his late eighties or early nineties. He had fought in World War II and the Korean War. He was an air force pilot. While fighting in the Battle of Inchon, in the Korean War, Peterson's plane malfunctioned and he crashed into a field. Everyone thought he would die, but Peterson pulled through and fully recovered. He went back to the United States with a shiny new plate in his head and a desk job.

Over the past three years, Tom had spent a lot of time talking with Peterson. Tom enjoyed listening to the old man's stories about growing up and his years in the military.

A few days after the couple moved into their new house, Brenda and Tom had a fight. Tom couldn't remember what it was about, but it was a bad one. As he was passing by Peterson's, he had been mumbling to himself.

The old man had overheard him and said, "Is everything okay, sonny?"

Not knowing why, Tom had walked up to Peterson and shared his troubles with him. Tom remembered what a beautiful summer day it had been. The two men sat at the picnic table for hours and talked. Peterson was a careful listener and wise. Peterson had never been married and didn't have any children.

Tom realized he should have been a little scared of the old man. Adam Peterson was at least six foot five and three hundred pounds, and his gray hair reached the middle of his back. His gray beard had at least three braids in it—along with some leftover breakfast.

Old Man Peterson wasn't the friendliest-looking fella or the most likely ally, but they had become very close. Tom had grown to love the old man very much.

Tom was halfway done digging out the Peterson house when the old man appeared, waving Tom off the tractor. "Shut that damn thing off, come inside, and warm yourself."

Tom jumped off the tractor and hugged his friend. "Looking good for an old fart," Tom said with a laugh.

Peterson thanked him and said, "Did you and the missus enjoy the lasagna I dropped off earlier this week?" After Donnie died, the old man had brought over a lasagna, bread, and salad.

"It was darn right tasty," Tom said. "We thank you from the bottom of our stomachs."

Peterson took two cups from the cupboard, poured himself a cup of coffee—adding a shot of brandy—and asked, "Want a little honey in your pot, son? It will take the edge off of today's events."

His first reaction was to decline, but instead, he said, "Hell yeah, Peterson. You might as well make it a double and forget the coffee. I will just take the honey."

"Why don't you just get on with it, Tom? What's on your mind, son?" Peterson raised a brow and tapped his fingers on the table.

Tom said, "If you stop that annoying tapping, I will tell you what is going on."

By the time he had finished telling his friend all that had happened, Peterson's face was red and filled with panic. "So, she doesn't know you are on to her?"

Before Tom could answer, they heard a crash on the side porch.

Tom looked out the window and saw Brenda's car in the driveway. He looked over at the side door and noticed that the screen was open. He rushed to the door and found a large, clay planter that had fallen off the railing and smashed into pieces. Beside the broken pot, there was a "Home Sweet Home" sign that had been poking out of that very same pot ever since Tom could remember.

On the walkway, Brenda was walking toward the door.

Tom was filled with a hot, overpowering dread. He felt faint and leaned against the wall to hide his horror. Had she heard their conversation? He knew he had to play it cool. "Hey, Bren. What in the world are you doing here?"

She looked dazed and had noticeable sweat beads on her face. "It is almost eleven thirty, honey. You said you wanted to be on the road by one o'clock. I figured you must have lost track of time. I know how you boys get to carrying on."

Tom took her gently by the arm, led her down the stairs, kissed her cheek, and put her back in her car. "You go on home and get everything ready to go. I am going to finish up here—and then I will be home. Should be half an hour or so. I love you."

She put the car in reverse and backed out of the driveway.

Tom could see Peterson looking out the window as he headed back in the house.

"Jesus," he shouted. "Do you think she heard us? Son, if she heard us, you could be in serious danger."

Tom poured more brandy into his cup and drank it down. "I don't think she heard us, Peterson. Anyway, I sure as hell hope she didn't." He hugged the old man and thanked him for his ear and the brandy.

"See you at the showing, son."

Tom went back outside, hopped on the tractor, and set off to finish the job he had started.

With his friend's house all cleaned up and dug out, Tom hurried home. It was time to get changed and head to Jackson for the showing.

When he pulled the tractor into his driveway, Brenda's car was gone. He drove the tractor around back, put it in the barn, and padlocked the door. He hurried into the house. *Where could she have possibly gone?*

He noticed a piece of paper taped to his bedroom door: "I have to run a few errands before we leave town. I will meet you at the funeral home at three o'clock. I ordered a lovely rose piece that says 'Son' on it. I will pick it up from the flower shop on my way. Also, Dillon has a runny nose and sounds like he is congested a bit. He might not make it through the long day. We should drive separately in case I have to bring him home. Love you—be careful. See you soon!"

Tom crumpled up the note and threw it into the garbage can. He wasn't the least bit surprised that she had left, and he felt sad that he was relieved she was gone.

The ride to Jackson took longer than he expected. He had not seen so much snow in years. He didn't pull down the long driveway until two forty-five. He was sure his parents would be anxious. They didn't like to be late and had made it their life's mission to always be on time.

His parents were coming out of the house when he pulled in.

Bernard walked up to him and said, "Son, just get on back in your truck. You are driving—and we are late."

Ruby looked around and asked, "Where is Brenda and our grandson?"

Tom sighed and said, "Get in. I will tell you about it on the way."

As they drove down the driveway, Tom told his parents about the note.

Bernard said, "Do you really care at this point, son? I just feel sorry for Dillon. Who knows what that crazy bitch is capable of. Tommy, you have to be careful. Maybe you should move out of that house. We fear for your safety."

Biting his thumbnail, he said, "Dad, I am a big boy. She isn't going to hurt me. I have to stay for now, Pop. Don't worry. I will be fine. I promise."

Tom pulled into the parking lot of the funeral home, and Bernard and Ruby got out. Tom parked in one of the spots reserved for family.

The outside of the funeral home was decorated with blue carnations, white roses, and yellow tulips. The landscape was breathtaking.

As Tom walked through the entrance, he saw his parents standing over a small casket. He paused for a moment, took a deep breath, and walked over to them.

The coffin was white with blue interior, and there was a beautiful arrangement of blue and white roses that read "Son" and "Grandson" on it. It was attached to the lid of the coffin.

Tom said, "Mom, did you order this piece for over the casket?"

With tears running down her face, she answered, "Yes, dear. I did. Isn't it magnificent?"

He wiped his eyes. "Yes, Mom. It is. Brenda is supposed

to pick up an arrangement. We will find a place for it when she gets here. Thank you so much for taking care of everything."

Ruby walked over to her son and wrapped her arms around him.

They held each other and cried for a few moments.

The entire first floor had been prepared for the funeral. Small-town folks stick together, and there would be many in attendance. Barton estimated the funeral would draw at least seven hundred people over the course of the two showings and the memorial service.

There was a lounge with a maximum occupancy of eighty people, one large, main viewing room with Donnie's little body, and two side viewing rooms. Flowers and plants bordered every room.

Tom said, "Barton, you and your staff have done a wonderful job. Thank you very much. Everything is beautiful."

Barton shook Tom's hand and said, "We are glad we are able to be here for you and your family during this time, son. Where is Brenda?"

Tom looked at his watch and said, "I don't know, Mr. Graves. She should have been here by now. I need to excuse myself and call her before people start to arrive. Pardon me." Tom was filled with panic as he dialed his wife's cell phone number. There was no answer. *Oh my God, Brenda. What the hell are you up to now?* He left a message for her to get to the funeral home right away or at least call him.

A lot of people were showing up to pay their respects. Tom did not realize he knew so many people, but there wasn't one person who hugged him or shook his hand who he didn't know by name. It was a good feeling to have so many people offer their support, and it was a great comfort.

He looked over at the entrance just as Brenda's parents, Michael and Fiona Miller, walked through the door.

Ruby saw them too and rushed over to greet them. Tom thought she must be up to something and hurried over to welcome his in-laws before his mother reached them.

Michael shook Tom's hand. "Michael, Fiona, so good of you to come. I am sorry you didn't get to meet our little Donnie. He was a precious angel."

"Our deepest sympathies, son." Michael Miller was the mayor of New Berry Falls. He was at the beginning of his second term and planned to go back to practicing law when his term was up since he could not run again. Michael was an honest man and enjoyed helping people. For the past twenty-five years, every Thanksgiving, Michael could be found at the Lutheran church, on the corner of East Avenue, serving turkey to those less fortunate. The Miller family's Thanksgiving feast was never held earlier than four o'clock for that reason.

Fiona Miller was a hospital administrator at Seneca Metro. She started working there as a candy striper when she was fifteen years old. She loved to help people and dedicated her life to the care of others.

Michael and Fiona were married a few weeks after their high school graduation and still seemed very much in love. Tom had always liked them both, and they seemed to like him too.

At a quarter to five, there was still no sign of Brenda. Tom asked Michael and Fiona to excuse him for a moment. He didn't mention that he couldn't find Brenda, and he thought it was strange that they had not asked him where their daughter was. He called her cell phone again, but he didn't leave a message this time.

Tom walked back into the main viewing room and rejoined Michael and Fiona.

Shaking his head, he asked, "Have either of you seen Brenda? She said she had some errands to run before the showing today. I called her cell phone twice with no luck."

Fiona said, "Sorry, Tom. We had a disagreement with Brenda on New Year's Eve and have not heard from her since. She didn't even call to tell us about Donnie. We read about it in the *Chronicle*. You can't imagine how horrified we were reading such news."

Tom shook his head and his face turned beet red. He had never questioned Brenda when she said she went to her parents' house the morning Donnie died. Never once did he think she would lie about it because it would have been too easy to check her story.

Michael put his hand on Tom's shoulder. "You all right, son? All of a sudden, you look sick."

"No. I am okay, Michael. I am sorry about Brenda. I didn't know anything about the disagreement. She hasn't been herself for quite some time."

Out of the corner of his eye, Tom saw the clock on the wall: five thirty. *Where could Brenda and Dillon be?* As he started out the door to call her again, she appeared in the doorway.

"Brenda!" Tom hugged her. "I am so glad you finally made it. Are you okay? Where have you been?"

She sat the baby carrier down as Tom helped her take off her coat. "We got a flat tire just outside of Canyon Heights. It took me forever to change the damn thing. Once I finally got the spare tire on and got on the road again, I looked for my cell phone and couldn't find it. I had to go back to where I changed the tire to see if I had dropped it. Sure enough, I dropped it out of my jacket pocket and ran it over when I took off." Brenda pulled the cell phone out of her coat pocket and presented it to her husband.

"I am so sorry, Bren. I was so worried. It's okay—you're here now."

She brushed the hair from her face and tried to straighten the creases on her skirt.

"The arrangement for Donnie is in the car, Tom. Could you please go out and get it for me?"

Tom took Dillon out of his carrier and handed him to his wife. "I will put Dillon's carrier in the coat room on my way out to your car." He dropped the carrier off and went outside. It was snowing again.

Tom unlocked Brenda's car and pulled back the passenger seat so he had room to lift out the arrangement without damaging it. When he pulled the seat back, he heard something fall from the car and hit the asphalt. He was horror-stricken when he looked down and saw the sign that belonged to Adam Peterson. Hours earlier, he had found it by the planter. Tom thought back to his visit with the old man and how he had said he would see Tom at the showing. He had not arrived yet. Another sickening feeling came over him.

He put the sign in his pocket and took the arrangement into the funeral home.

At seven thirty, Brenda told Tom she was taking Dillon home. The baby hadn't stopped sneezing or coughing since they arrived, and Tom agreed it was a good idea for them to start home, especially with the snow coming down again. With Dillon bundled up, Tom walked his wife and son to the car. After kissing them both, he shut the door.

As Brenda drove off, he put his hand into his pocket and found the sign. He went off to tell his parents what he had found in Brenda's car.

Ruby and Bernard were in the coffee lounge with Barton—and a bottle of brandy.

"Can you please pour me a little of that, Barton?" Tom was shaking as he grabbed a coffee cup from the cupboard.

They waved goodbye to Barton and headed for the farm.

"Okay," Ruby said. "Do you want to tell me why you were shaking like a leaf when you came into the coffee lounge and asked for booze?"

Tom explained how he had gone to the car for the arrangement and what he had found. Pulling the sign out of his pocket, he held it up for the parents to see.

Bernard said, "That came out of the planter that fell at Peterson's house? I don't get it. Why did she have it—and when did she get it?"

Tom pulled over to the side of the road and turned around so he could look at his father in the back seat. "Dad, it means Brenda went back to Peterson's house after I left. Maybe that is really why she was late."

They all sat in silence for some time.

Tom snapped out of thought and pulled the truck back onto the road.

Arriving back at the farm, Tom decided to head home. He was anxious to go by Peterson's house to check on him. "I will be back tomorrow morning—no later than eight. I might as well eat breakfast with you two before heading back to the funeral home. With Dillon's cold getting worse, I highly doubt Brenda will make an appearance at the funeral tomorrow. To be honest, I'd prefer if she stayed home."

Bernard and Ruby got out of the truck and headed inside.

Tom turned down Route 55 at nine thirty. As he got closer to his house, he noticed a strange orange glow in the sky. When he pulled into his driveway he could see what was causing the illumination. Peterson's barns, house, and land were on fire!

Brenda ran out of the house. "Tom! Oh my God, Tom! When Dillon and I got home, there were fire trucks and police cars all over. We had a hell of a time getting into our driveway. I didn't want to call and upset you—or take a chance of you getting into a wreck speeding home with worry. I heard on the police scanner that Adam was taken to the hospital with third-degree burns on most of his body. I am so sorry, baby. They are still trying to put out the fire." Brenda took Tom's hand as he stared at the flames and smoke.

He shook her hand off his, jumped back in his truck, and headed to Peterson's place. The police had blocked off the road at least two hundred yards on each side of the entrance. Tom parked his truck on the side of the road and walked toward the house.

Detective Shae Tomkins was standing by one of the four fire trucks.

Tom walked up to the detective and shook his hand.

"Nice to see you again," Shae said. "I am sorry we are meeting under these circumstances. Are you and Adam Peterson friends?"

Tom shook his head. "Yes, we are very close. He is like a father to me. What happened? I left him at twelve fifteen this afternoon. He said he would see me at the funeral home—and then he never showed up."

Shae was taking notes as Tom spoke. "The fire was reported by a young man who drove by and saw the flames. I was told by the chief that the fire department got the call at 4:20 this afternoon and arrived here at 4:35. The flames had already engulfed all the barns and the house and was spreading to the fields when they arrived. The fire had to have been burning for a while before it was spotted and reported. I would think your wife would have seen the glow from a raging fire like this one. They found Mr. Peterson right there. Adam was taken by ambulance to the hospital. He had suffered third-degree burns over 90 percent of his body. I just feel awful about it all. That old man is one hell of a nice fella."

Tom's eyes were filled with tears, and his face was hot from the heat of the flames. "Does anyone know what could have caused a fire like this?" Tom was shaking as he waited for a reply from the detective.

Shae looked up from his notepad. "Not yet. Nothing can be done until the flames are out and the entire site has cooled. It will take a day or so, and then we will conduct an extensive and thorough investigation. I have very little experience with fires. I am not a fireman, but in my opinion, based on cases I have read about and chemistry class, this fire was fueled by gas or some chemical. It is a class b fire. It covered such a large area and burned so damn hot. Plus, I located three industrial-sized propane tanks on the property."

Tom said, "The propane tanks were used to fuel the sprinklers for the grain fields."

The detective's cell phone rang. "Detective Tomkins here. I am sorry to hear that. I will take care of notifying the family."

Tom had a terrible feeling he knew what the phone call was about. "Peterson is dead, isn't he?"

Shae shook his head. "Yes. Mr. Peterson was pronounced dead ten minutes ago. I am sorry for the loss of your friend. Do you have the name and number of his sister? She will need to be notified right away. I know he wasn't married and didn't have any children."

Tom was devastated. He couldn't believe his friend was

**TAMI BOYER**

gone. His thoughts drifted to the sign in Brenda's car. Tom couldn't help but think she had killed his best friend, and he blamed himself. Should he tell Detective Tomkins about his suspicions? After all, they were only suspicions—or were they? How many more people were going to die before he talked to the police?

Did Brenda kill the old man to keep him from telling someone about his conversation with Tom? If she had killed Peterson, what would she do to Tom? He had been there too.

"Tom? You okay?" Detective Tomkins waved a hand in front of Tom's face, attempting to snap him out of the trance he was in.

"Yes, yes, I am fine. Sorry, I was lost in thought about my friend for a moment. If it is okay with you and the CHPD, I would prefer to contact Peterson's sister myself. Her name is Joanne Roberts. She teaches fifth grade at McKinley Heights Elementary. They were very close. I think it would be better if I told her."

Shae said, "I don't see what harm it would cause, Tom. Thank you for taking the time to contact her. Please give me a call once she has been notified."

Tom shook the detective's hand. "I am going to go over to her house now. Don't think it wise to wait until the morning. She may hear it on the news before I have the chance to tell her. I also don't think a phone call will suffice in this situation either. Ever since Joanne's husband, Danny, died in that wreck last year, she has not been the most emotionally stable woman. I know just how to handle Jo Jo. We have been friends for a few years now. Thank you for letting me take care of this. I will talk to you later this evening."

Tom pulled into Joanne's driveway at ten fifteen, and the lights were still on. He got out of his truck and started up the front sidewalk.

The porch light came on, and Joanne opened the door. "Tommy Sherrill, what in the world are you doing here at this late hour?" Joanne was wearing a pink silk nightgown. The light from the hallway revealed the curves of her intoxicating body. Her light gray hair was long and soft. She was an elegant woman. Tom thought she was beautiful and always held a special place in his heart for her. Telling Joanne that Peterson was dead was very hard for him. He loved her.

"Hey, Jo Jo. Sorry to bother you so late, but there is something I gotta tell ya and it can't wait until morning. May I come in?" Tom was tired and pale.

"Of course. Please come in. May I get you some coffee?"

He walked through the door, took off his coat, and hung it up. "Yes, that would be nice. I could use some coffee."

Joanne put two cups, a coffeepot, cream, sugar, and some Girl Scout cookies on a tray and placed the tray on the coffee table. "Tom, please sit. I can see you are very upset. What is it you want to speak to me about?"

He sat next to Joanne on the couch and poured himself a cup of coffee. "It is Adam," Tom said. "His entire property went up in flames tonight. When I left his place to come here, the fire department was still fighting the flames. Detective Shae Tomkins was on the scene. He said he thought the fire may have been caused by the three propane tanks Peterson used to power the irrigation system."

She dropped her head and began to cry. "Poor Adam. He must be a wreck about losing everything in the fire. That land has been in our family for more than a hundred years. He has to be devastated. How is my brother handling this, Tom? Where is he?"

Tom looked up from his coffee cup and took Joanne's hand. "When I got to Adam's place tonight, the detective told me he had been taken to the hospital. He was burned pretty badly, according to what the fire chief told the detective. I am so sorry, Joanne, but Adam is dead. Detective Shae got the phone call from the hospital when we were talking at the scene. I am so sorry, honey." Tom took her into his arms and held her while she cried and screamed for her only brother.

"Where is he now, Tom? At the hospital morgue? Will there be an autopsy?" Joanne wiped her eyes on the sleeve of her nightgown.

"Detective Tomkins asked that I call him after I spoke with you. I will call him to let him know we have had our talk and see what he suggests we do next. Okay?"

She nodded. "Thank you for being here, Tom. I don't know what I would do if you weren't."

He kissed her forehead and excused himself to make his call. After a brief conversation with the detective, Tom went back into the living room.

Joanne was crying on the couch. She looked up when he walked into the room. "Do we have to go to the hospital to identify Adam body?"

Shae had suggested Tom go alone to *officially* identify Peterson's body. It was so badly burned that the detective didn't want Joanne to see her brother's body in such a condition. "No. There is no need to go to the hospital, Joanne. The fire chief identified him on the scene when they found him. He held his hand the whole time, Joanne. Adam wasn't alone." Tom would go down to the morgue when he finished up with Joanne and identify Peterson's body. He knew Peterson would not want the last image his sister had of him to be his dead, burned body.

"There will be an autopsy on Monday. Not real sure why they would perform an autopsy. The cause of death was obviously the fire. Guess it's good to be sure. The body will be ready for release on Monday afternoon. I know Adam didn't want a funeral or showing—only to be cremated and scattered over the family land. He left a box with me, six months ago, that has all of his important papers in it. He told me you have the key. I can come by tomorrow after Donnie's memorial service, and we can look at them together if you want."

She stood up and hugged Tom. "Oh, you poor, dear. You lost your son, and here I am going on and on. I planned to come to the showing and the memorial service tomorrow. You will understand if I don't make the trip under the circumstances? All my love to you and Brenda, sweetie. You also lost your dear friend today. I thank you for all the time you spent with Adam. He loved you like a son."

"Thank you, Joanne. That means a lot to me. I loved him too—very much. I wouldn't expect you to make the drive with everything that has happened. I will be here around suppertime tomorrow. We can get some dinner and look over the papers then. Let me know if you need anything in the meantime."

When Tom pulled into the hospital parking lot, Detective Tomkins was waiting for him. They shook hands and went inside.

In the morgue, the detective turned to Tom and said, "There is not much left of Mr. Peterson as you can imagine with third degree burns covering 98 percent of his body. We are hoping you will be able to identify him by any of the distinguishing items or marks on the body that are still visible. You will want to hold your breath when the coroner's assistant opens the cold-storage locker. The smell is very unpleasant and will very likely make you vomit. Whenever you're ready, we will proceed."

Tom took a deep breath. "Let's do this, Detective Tomkins. I am ready."

The two men walked into a bright room that looked like it went on for miles. The ceiling was painted white, and the walls and floors were white tile except for one wall. The wall that was not tiled was row after row of cold-storage lockers where the bodies awaiting identification and/or autopsy were stored. The room was cold and eerie. Tom thought the room must be filled with the ghosts of all the people who had laid in the boxes before.

The assistant opened up one of the lockers and asked Tom to step forward as he lifted the plastic sheet. It was a horrible sight—unreal and unimaginable.

There was a metal plate on the left side of the corpse's head. Tom shook his head. "Yes. This is Adam Peterson. That is the metal plate that was put in his head after his plane went down in the Battle of Inchon, during the Korean War." Tom pointed to the plate as he wiped the tears from his eyes.

The assistant zipped the black bag and closed the locker. The assistant handed Tom a piece of paper and told him that, in signing it, he was identifying the corpse in locker 56 as Adam Peterson.

He signed the paper and set the pen on the desk. "I need to get going now. Donnie's memorial service is tomorrow, and I have to try to get a few hours of sleep. Please call me with any questions you may have, Detective Tomkins."

Tom got in his truck and headed home. He thought about going to a hotel or even staying at the farm, but he needed to check on his family and sleep in his own bed. The past week had been devastating, and he was confused. It was like he was in a bad dream and couldn't wake up. Tom had lost his son and his best friend. Could Brenda be responsible for Peterson's death too? He could not conceive that she would have set that fire. The woman he married could never kill anyone, but she wasn't that beautiful girl he met at Kaila's Place so many years ago. If she was capable of killing a defenseless infant, she was capable of anything as far as he was concerned. He would wait to hear from Detective Tomkins in regard to the cause of the fire. If it was ruled arson, he would go to the detective and tell him everything, including the facts involving Donnie's death. If the cause was a propane leak or something that was not caused by another person, he would continue waiting and watching.

When Tom walked into the house, there were no lights on. He figured Brenda must have gone to bed. In the kitchen, he turned on the light—and Brenda was sitting at the table in the dark. She had a crazed look on her face, and her hair was wet with what appeared to be sweat. She didn't acknowledge his presence. She acted like she was under a spell, and it scared the hell out of him.

"Brenda, you okay?"

No answer.

Tom went over to where she was sitting and touched her hand. "Bren, are you all right? Brenda!" Tom's voice was loud and full of fear.

She nodded and looked at him. "Oh, hi, honey. I have been waiting up for you. How is Mr. Peterson? Are you all right, my love?"

He sat down next to his wife and took her hand in his. He let out a breath and rolled his head back and forth to crack his neck.

Her skin was so soft, and she smelled like the rose lotion he bought her for Christmas. He looked down at her hand and saw what looked like a burn on her palm. It was read and inflamed.

"Peterson is dead—98 percent of his body was burnt.

He suffered terribly. I went over to Joanne Roberts's house tonight to tell her the bad news. Then I went down to the hospital morgue to identify him. Detective Tomkins and I thought it would be better for her, emotionally, if she wasn't the person who identified him. It was horrible, and the smell was sickening. I can't believe two people I love are dead in less than a week." Tom put his head in his hands and sobbed uncontrollably for several minutes.

Brenda did not console him, touch him, or ask if there was anything she could do. She looked at him with a deranged grin.

He wanted to reach out and smack her across her face. He wiped the tears from his eyes and took her hand in his again. "Bren, is there anything you want to tell me or talk about? You know you can tell me anything, right?" He rubbed the area on her hand that looked like a burn.

She jumped. "Damn it, Tom! Why did you do that?" She ran to the sink, turned on the cold water, and put her hand under the faucet.

"What is that on your hand—and how did you get it? And where did the sign in your car come from? It fell out when I pulled back the passenger seat to get the arrangement. The sign looks exactly like the sign that fell out of a planter that broke this morning at Peterson's house. What the fuck is going on with you, Brenda?"

She turned off the water and stared out the window for a few moments. Her eyes were black and lifeless. She opened the drawer next to the sink, took out a clean dish towel, and wrapped her hand in it. "I got the burn yesterday when I made cookies for you. You know how I rush around the kitchen. I reached in without a potholder for heaven's sake. It hurts like hell! As far as the sign is concerned, I picked it up last week when I bought the rubber tree." Brenda pointed to a plant in front of the dining room window. "You made fun of it when I brought it home, remember? You made a few nasty jokes and said it was ugly. I thought I lost my little sign. Thank you so much for finding it. May I have it please?"

Tom took the sign out of his pocket and handed it to her. "What about the way I found you sitting here in the dark, Bren? What is that all about? You looked like a crazy woman."

Before she could answer, Dillon began screaming from the master bedroom.

Tom ran into the room to see what was troubling his son. Brenda followed behind him.

When he opened the door, he could hear the dehumidifier and smell menthol in the air.

Brenda rushed to the baby and picked him up. "I was worried about this little guy. After we left the funeral home, he started crying and screaming. I couldn't settle him down by talking to him. I pulled over so I could cradle and soothe him. When I picked him up, his skin was very hot. I knew he had a fever, and it scared me, especially with already losing Donnie. Oh, God. I can't lose another son. I took him to the emergency room, and the doctor said he has pneumonia. I was covered in water from the ice I packed for him. The doctor said it was the best chance for reducing his fever. I stopped at Gracie's Mini Mart on the way home from the emergency room and got forty pounds of ice. The clerk loaded it in the trunk for me. I wanted to tell you when you got home from the funeral home, but things were frenzied with the fire and Mr. Peterson's death. I didn't get a chance to tell you."

Tom gently rubbed his son's back. "Poor little guy. I have been so wrapped up in Donnie's death and the Peterson tragedy that I didn't remember you had the sniffles. Daddy is so sorry, Dillon."

Brenda handed him the baby. "My two favorite men in the whole wide world. Isn't he precious, Tom?"

He had not had any time to enjoy being a father for a week. His thoughts drifted back to Donnie. "Is it safe to say you will need to stay home tomorrow with Dillon? He obviously can't come to the funeral home with pneumonia." Tom handed the baby back to Brenda.

Dillon buried his head in her chest and drifted off to sleep.

It was a lovely sight, and Tom would have enjoyed it so much more if he didn't feel so much contempt for his wife.

"One of us will need to stay with him. I assumed it would be me, but if you prefer to stay home with Dillon, honey, that is fine too. I will go put Donnie down to rest." Her words made him sick to his stomach. How could she even think he would let her go to the funeral home instead of him? He knew she had heard his conversation with Peterson.

"No, honey. You stay with Dillon. Everyone wants their mommy when they are sick. I will take care of the memorial service. Mom and Dad will be there to help me. They have been such a wonderful help. I am going to go on up to bed now. I feel like I am going to fall over, and my head feels like it is going to explode. Love you." After kissing Brenda and Dillon, Tom headed upstairs to bed. Once inside his bedroom, he closed the door and locked it.

The next morning, Tom awoke to the sound of someone trying to open his bedroom door. He looked at the clock: 5:57. The doorknob turned and jiggled.

"Hello? Brenda?"

No answer.

He looked at the crack under the door and saw a shadow

moving back and forth. He got out of bed and opened the door, but nobody was there. He looked down the hall just in time to see the master bedroom door close.

He got dressed, brushed his teeth, found a suitcase in his closet, and filled it with as many clothes and personal belongings as the case would hold. Tom was in no mood for games and decided to take off for the farm before Brenda got up. He didn't feel safe in his home any longer. He grabbed his keys and headed for the farm.

His parents' house smelled like syrup and coffee. How he missed waking up to such marvelous smells in the morning. "Good morning! Your favorite son is home!" Tom took off his coat and hung it up by the door.

Ruby popped her head into the living room. "Come on in, son. Breakfast is ready."

He kissed his mom on the cheek. "Morning, Mommy. Where is Pop?"

She touched his cheek lovingly. "He will be down in a couple minutes. Where is Brenda and my grandson?"

Tom sat down at the table and poured himself a cup of coffee. "Dillon has pneumonia, and Brenda is at home with him. I am glad that Brenda is not here, Mom. I am so sad to say that, but I am damn glad she is not coming today." Tom put his head in his hands and began to cry. "When I got home last night, there were fire trucks and police cars down the road at the Peterson farm. He is dead, Mom."

Ruby sat down next to her son. "What are you talking about? What are you saying? What happened?"

Bernard walked into kitchen and said, "Good morning, son. You look tired. No sleep last night?"

Tom looked up at his dad and shook his head. "Sit down, Pop. I was just getting ready to tell Mom what happened last night." Tom told them everything.

Bernard got up from the table and put his hands on the counter. "Why in the hell didn't you call us last night? You should have turned your truck around and come straight back here, Tom. What in God's name were you thinking? You can't stay in that house, boy. You are in danger."

Ruby got up from her chair and put her arm around Bernard. "He's right, son. I think you should stay here for a while—just until you figure out what to do. You need to mourn the loss of your son and your best friend. In that house, you will never have any peace. You will be watching your back every minute. Please consider moving in here for a little while. I am so afraid for you, Tommy."

He looked at his mom and then his dad. "I was thinking that would be a good idea. I packed a suitcase this morning. It is in my truck. I can't go back there. I woke up this morning to the doorknob on my bedroom door turning. The door was locked. When I called out, there was no answer. When I looked out the door, I saw the master bedroom door closing. It was creepy—like something out of a scary movie. Brenda was up to something this morning. Good thing my door was locked."

Bernard sat down next to his son. "Listen, kid. If that crazy bitch is responsible for Peterson's death, you are in serious danger. I am afraid I have to insist you go to that detective you spoke about and tell him what in the hell has been going on. Do it—or I will."

Tom closed his eyes for a few moments and sighed. He wondered how much one person could take before having a mental breakdown. "Detective Tomkins said he would call me when they had concluded what caused the fire. The site needs a day or two to cool down before they can begin their investigation. He also said he would let me know the official cause of death. It is pretty obvious from looking at his terribly burned body. I have never seen anything like that before. That picture will haunt me for the rest of my life." His head hung low as he sobbed.

Ruby wiped the tears from her eyes and went over to her son. "Okay. We need to get to the funeral home. Let's put everything else aside for the afternoon. We need to focus on the memorial service and saying our goodbyes to Donnie."

At least three hundred people showed up to pay their respects at the funeral home. Reverend Holt made the trip from Canyon Heights and delivered a beautiful service in memory of Donnie.

As usual, Kaila prepared a wonderful deli lunch, complete with several different pastries. A hundred people stayed to eat.

Tom thought about taking a plate to Brenda, but he decided not to since there wasn't much left. And he wasn't going home after the service. He was going to meet Joanne to open the box that contained Peterson's will. Joanne had the key to the box.

He planned to head back to the farm after their meeting.

After the last paper plate and plastic fork was picked up, Tom sat down at the table and took a flask of whiskey from his jacket pocket. He looked around at the people in the church basement. "Everyone, please come over and join me in a toast." Tom took five plastic cups and poured a shot in each.

His parents, Barton, and Reverend Holt all took a cup. "Thank you all for being here. Please help me toast my son and best friend. To Donnie, my son, you weren't on this earth very long, but I am glad for the short time we shared together. I love you, my boy. To Adam Peterson, my, dear friend. Thank you for being the cool old man you were. I will never forget you."

They all raised their cups and drank their shots.

"That's it then. Time to go." He hugged Ruby, shook the men's hands, and threw the cups in the recycling bag. "I will take this bag out on my way to the truck. I have to drive back to Canyon Heights to meet with Joanne, and then I will be back, Mom. Okay?"

Ruby waved to him. "See you soon, Tommy. Be safe!"

Tom pulled into Joanne's driveway. He took Peterson's box from the passenger seat and walked to the front door.

Joanne opened the door and greeted him. "Hi, Tom. I'm glad to see you. How was the service?"

Tom kissed her cheek and smiled. "It was beautiful. I was so glad to see people I had not seen in a long time. Too bad it takes a funeral to put old friends back in touch. How are you, honey? Did you get any sleep last night?"

Joanne smiled. "Yes, that is too bad indeed, but it is a great feeling to reconnect with old friends. I slept about four hours last night. Hanging in there I guess. I sure am hungry though. Let's check out the old man's will and go get some dinner. Sound good to you?"

He put Peterson's box on the coffee table. "Yes. That sounds wonderful. I am starving and could use a stiff drink."

Joanne sat down next to him and put the key on top of the box. "You open it, Tom. I can't do it."

He picked up the key, put it in the lock, and turned it. When he opened the lid, he smelled a familiar odor. They looked in the box and saw a bottle of the old man's favorite cologne: Old Spice.

Joanne and Tom laughed when they saw the bottle and were so happy to enjoy the smell again. They each told a Peterson story and then looked back into the box. There was only one other item in the box, and it was a single piece of paper. Tom took it out of the box and unfolded it. The will was simply written. Peterson did not want a showing or a burial. He was to be cremated and his ashes spread around the big, old oak tree out by the pond at the back of the Peterson property. He didn't want anyone at the ash spreading except Joanne and Tom. Peterson was very clear about keeping the affair simple and easy. The 150 acres of land was to be divided between his sister and best friend. Tom was to inherit he front sixty acres with the house and barns. Joanne got the back ninety acres with the pond.

"I am so glad you and I will be taking care of Adam greatest passion—the Peterson land. He loved you so much, Tom. He talked about you like a son. It will be a pleasure to share the land with you, my dear friend." She hugged him and kissed his cheek.

"I figured something was up with the old fart when he left the box with me and the key with you. Do you know what Peterson told me when I asked him why the hell he wasn't using the brand-new snow blower you bought him?"

She thought about it for a moment and shook her head.

"He said he didn't want to use that snow blower because his precious little sister bought it for him—and he didn't want to mess it up."

She smiled and shook her head. "Sounds like Adam. He was my biggest fan, and I was his. Ya don't see a lot of siblings as close as the two of us. I sure am glad the good Lord blessed me with such a wonderful brother. He was one of a kind. He also brought you into my life. I am very grateful for that, Tommy. If you hadn't been walking past Adam's place that day, mumbling to yourself, you wouldn't be here for me today. Yeah, he told me about that. Do you think he wouldn't have mentioned it to me? We had the best laugh when he told that story. I can still see the joy in his eyes and his big belly shaking as he laughed. I don't know how I will get through each day without him in it." Tears fell from Joanne's eyes.

Tom didn't remember feeling so badly for another human being. Adam would be distraught to see his big sister suffering.

Joanne wiped her face with the sleeve of her blouse. "Anyway, I am glad to have you in my life, Tom. I couldn't bear any of this if you weren't here. You were so good to me when I lost Danny. I enjoyed the time we spent together. It was a wonderful distraction from reality." She took Tom's hand and looked deep into his eyes, "Thank you, Tom. From the bottom of my heart, you really are the nicest, most honest fella I have ever met." Joanne hugged Tom.

Tom pulled away from her hug just enough to look into her eyes. He seemed concerned. "Are you okay?"

"I am good … just a little tired … missing Adam. Would you like to meet me at the farm tomorrow? I really need to be closer to Adam. I was thinking around ten in the morning if that works for you. Being Sunday and all, I would normally be sitting in a pew at church with Adam right alongside me—been that way for the past thirty years, but I can't bear to go without him. Plus, there is so much to do out there. He would be so bent out of shape with all that mess. I will feel closer to him there. What do you think? Are you in?"

Tom hugged Joanne and said, "Yes, I will be there at ten o'clock sharp. I wouldn't miss it. I need to be where he would be."

"Okay then. I will bring the fixings for a nice picnic. Would you feel okay being in charge of bringing the wine? Whatever you bring will be fine. I am easy. Well, I am not picky that is."

Tom laughed, "I am all over it, Jo Jo. I think we will need

a few drinks with that mess. Please be prepared, dear, the place is pretty burned up."

She stepped away from Tom, walked to the window, and looked outside. "I figured as much. I hope some of Adam's antiques, anything that was his, can be salvaged. Oh, Tom." The tears began to fall from her eyes.

"I should say good night if that is okay with you. I want to get up and finish all my chores early so I can get out to the farm." Tom walked to the door, and she followed behind him. Kissing her softly on the cheek, Tom said, "Good night, sweets. Try to get some sleep."

She shut her eyes for a moment. "'Night Tommy, until tomorrow."

Back in his truck, Tom's thoughts drifted to the events of the past week. He wondered when he was going to be able to exhale. He hoped he could sneak into the house without waking up his folks. Tom was too tired to hang out and chat. He loved every minute he got with his mom and dad, but he was anxious to get to bed so he could get out to the farm and get to work. He was glad for the distraction—but sad at how it came to him.

Walking up to the front door, Tom could tell Barton and Ruby were asleep. He opened the door and walked quietly to his room. Tom undressed down to his boxers, got in bed, pulled the covers over his head, and turned off the light. He was asleep before his head hit the pillow.

Hitting the off button on his alarm clock, Tom said, "I hate that sound. Six o'clock already? Yuck!"

He threw off the covers and got out of bed. He could smell the fresh coffee coming from the kitchen. He got dressed, cleaned up, brushed his teeth, and went downstairs for a big cup of wake-up coffee.

Ruby was scooping hash browns into a frying pan. "Good morning, darling."

Tom kissed her cheek.

Ruby put a cup of coffee on the table as he sat down.

"Morning, Ma. I slept better last night than I have in such a long time. I feel very rested and alert. Thank you so much for inviting me to stay with you guys."

Ruby took a seat beside her son and put her hand on his face. "This will always be your home, honey. You are welcome here anytime, day or night, now and always."

"Thanks, Mom. I am so lucky to have the support of the two best parents in the world."

Bernard stomped down the stairs and said, "Good morning, family. What are your plans today, son?" He kissed Ruby on the cheek, patted Tom on the shoulder, and sat at the head of the table like he had for as long as Tom could remember.

"I am going to head over to the Peterson farm at seven thirty. Joanne and I are meeting at ten to see how much is left of the place. When I got home last night, you guys were asleep. I wasn't able to tell you what Adam left to me in his will. A while back, he gave me lockbox and asked me to keep it for him. He said the box held his 'last will and testament.' He gave the key to Joanne, and if anything should ever happen to him, we were to open the box together. Well, last night we opened the box—and what a surprise we got. That old fart left me the land the house and barns sit on, roughly sixty acres. He left the back ninety acres with the pond to Joanne. We are going to start cleaning up the mess. Peterson would be so unhappy with the condition over there. We felt it was a worthy way to honor him by getting the land he loved so much put back together. Long road, we know, but it will be good to be close to him and his true love: his land."

Ruby said, "Aren't you afraid you will run into Brenda?"

Tom's cell phone rang, and it was Brenda. "Speak of the devil." Tom ignored it, deciding he wasn't going to let her piss him off so early in the morning.

"Have you decided what you are going to do about her, son?" Bernard was spreading strawberry jam on a warm biscuit.

"Obviously, we are not going to have a happy ending, Pop, but I have to stay long enough to prove she murdered my son and best friend. I know I am not responsible for Donnie's death, but I feel 100 percent responsible for Peterson's death. If I hadn't opened my big-ass mouth, I would be heading over there for coffee this morning. We had coffee together every Sunday after church. This is the first time without our Sunday coffee since he had his hip replacement two years ago. We still had our coffee that day, but it was in the hospital." Tears fell from Tom's eyes as he got up from the table. "Well, Ma, that was a super breakfast. Thank you very much. I think I will head out while the weather is good. I heard we could get four to six inches today. And yes, Mom, I promise to head back before the weather turns bad."

Bernard said, "Thanks, son. You be safe. We love you."

Tom shook Bernard's hand and kissed his mom on the top of her head.

Ruby grabbed his hand as he walked away. "Son, you be careful over there. Stay away from Brenda. That woman means to harm you. I got one of my bad feelings, baby. You know my feelings always end up being right. Damn them to hell, but they do."

When Tom turned to walk out of the room, a cold chill went up his spine.

# FALLING  DOWN

The road back to Canyon Heights was clear, and Tom arrived at Peterson's at eight forty-five. When he got out of his truck, he couldn't believe the charred mess. There wasn't too much left of the house—except for the kitchen and root cellar. Adam had made the kitchen into a makeshift nuclear fallout shelter not too long after he came home from the war.

When Tom would tease him about the steel walls, cupboards, counters, and table, Adam said, "Hey, kid, you weren't in Korea. And thank God for that because we would have been in big trouble."

Tom smiled. "Only Peterson." He was determined to check out the barns before Joanne arrived. As he approached the first barn, Brenda pulled up in the driveway. She got out of the car and ran toward him. She stormed up to him with her fists clenched at her side. "So, what, now you are divorcing me, Tom? You are such a coward running off to your mommy and daddy. Just like always—little mama's boy! You are a weakling, Tom! I knew it when I met you! You will always be a pussy!"

Tom grabbed her arm. "Where is Dillon, Brenda? And who in the hell do you think you are, coming at me like this? You have yourself to blame for all of this. Up until this moment, I was unsure exactly what I should do about our troubled marriage, but after this display, I am over it. I am filing for divorce tomorrow, Brenda. I am not a pussy, but you are a crazy bitch! What really happened with Donnie—huh, Brenda? And Peterson. Do you really think I believe that was an accident? You heard us talking and decided to get rid of him. Didn't you? What about me, Bren? You gonna kill me too?"

Her face turned completely white, and her nose curled up. "Dillon is with my parents in New Berry Falls. He is staying the night. I was certain you would come home and we could work things out. But if this is how you want things, Tom Sherrill, then fine. Fuck you!" She stormed away, mumbling to herself.

*Brenda is a murderer. Oh my god! What in the hell am I going to do now?* He felt dizzy and nauseous. *What am I going to do?* He decided to head back to the house and wait for Joanne. He didn't feel good enough to explore anymore by himself. Knowing how ungraceful he was, Tom felt it best to sit safely at the kitchen table where he and his friend had pondered life on so many occasions.

When he walked into the kitchen, he heard a cat meow. Walking over to the edge, where there was no more floor, he concluded the cat was in the root cellar. He got a little closer to the edge and saw the cat run across the floor of the root cellar. The cat was Peterson's pal Cooper. Tom had given him to his friend for Christmas two years ago. The two were inseparable. Cooper followed Adam everywhere he went. Tom hadn't even thought about Cooper. He felt bad about that fact and was looking for a way to get down to the root cellar.

He tried calling the cat to see if he might jump up to the kitchen floor, but there was really no way for Cooper to get himself out. "That is a long way down, fella," Tom said. He had forgotten that the house was actually four stories: the root cellar, the ground-level floor, the attic, and the subattic. About fifteen years ago, Peterson decided he wanted a "viewing tower." It was half the size of the attic and reminded Tom of the top tier of a wedding cake. The Victorian house had been built in 1810 and was a historic landmark.

Out of the corner of his eye, he saw a dark shadow moving. Suddenly, there was a loud shriek. Brenda was running toward him with her arms out in front of her and screaming like a crazy woman.

Tom had no time to get out of the way and nowhere to go but down. He knew what was about to happen, and he wasn't scared. The only thing he could think about was surviving so he could be sure Brenda was held accountable for killing Donnie and Peterson. Tom tried to brace himself for the impact of hitting the cellar floor below.

Brenda looked down at the cellar floor and looked around frantically to see if there was a way to get down there. "You have to be dead," she said. She looked around the kitchen and picked up several boards and other charred pieces of wood. She began dragging the wood over to the end of the steel floor and pushing them over the edge. With each piece she pushed over the side, she smiled and laughed. When she saw only the top of Tom's head, an arm, and his feet, Brenda wiped herself off and headed back to her car.

When Joanne arrived at the Peterson farm, she could tell that Tom was already there. She glanced at the clock on the dashboard of her 1958 Plymouth and saw it was 10:34. She was four minutes late. She paused for a moment, laughed, and said, "Maybe I will get a spanking. Shame on you, girl."

She got out of the car, and her smile quickly turned to a frown when she saw what was left of the farm. There was no sign of Tom. Near the house, she could hear a cat meowing. The closer she got to the house, the louder the meowing got. When she entered the kitchen, half the floor was gone. She looked over the edge and saw Tom. Cooper was resting on Tom's chest. "Oh my God! Tom! Can you hear me?"

There was no answer.

She took out her phone and called 911.

The paramedics arrived first, followed closely by two fire trucks and a few police cars.

Joanne was kneeling by the edge of the floor and looking down at Tom when the emergency professionals entered the kitchen. They asked her to step aside and quickly began rigging safety lines with a basket. One of the firemen climbed onto the basket and was lowered down to the floor of the root cellar. The lines were pulled to the surface, and another fireman climbed on. Soon, five firemen were pulling wood and other debris off of Tom.

Cooper was brought to the surface, and Joanne pulled the scared feline to her chest. He looked like he hadn't eaten in days. She rubbed his ear and whispered, "Thank you for letting me know he was down there. Thank you so much. I will get some food in your belly soon, Cooper—just hold on a little longer." She heard the jingling of the lines and saw that Tom was being raised to the surface.

The paramedics jumped in and took over.

Tom's head was covered in blood, and it looked like his head was twice its usual size. The four-inch laceration on his forehead looked very serious. There was blood seeping from both ears. The EMTs put him on a gurney and rushed him into the ambulance.

Joanne decided to take Cooper to her place. She would feed him and make him comfortable before going to the hospital to be with Tom. She let the paramedics know she would be close behind them.

The ambulance sped off, sirens blaring.

She rushed to her car and dropped her keys along the way. As she bent down to pick them up, Detective Tomkins said, "Mrs. Roberts, may I speak with you for a moment?"

"Do you mind meeting me at the hospital, Officer? I am going to drop Adam's cat at my house and then go to the hospital. Would you mind? I am sorry for the bother."

Shae opened the car door for Joanne and stroked Cooper's tail. "No problem, Mrs. Roberts. I will see you at the hospital in a little bit. I won't take much of your time. I only need to ask you a few routine questions since you are the person who found Tom. I am so sorry about your friend."

Joanne nodded, shut her door, and drove off. On the way to her house, she thought about calling Brenda to let her know what had happened to Tom. She decided to wait until she got to the hospital so she actually had some news about his condition. Joanne pulled into her driveway and ran up the stairs as quickly as she could. "You sure don't miss many meals, Cooper. I think I will have to put you on low-fat kitty food, but for tonight, you can have some of Patches's food. She is my precious angel. You two will get along wonderfully. For now, I am gonna lock her in my room until I have time to properly introduce you." Joanne opened the front door and put Cooper in the bathroom while she went to collect Patches. Joanne knew exactly where to find Patches: in the picture window on the landing of the stairs. "Gotcha, sweetie. Mommy has to put you in her bedroom for a little bit." She placed the cat in the screened window and went downstairs to get her water dish. She would run home and introduce the cats in a few hours. They would both be fine until then.

After placing the water on the floor next to the closet and showing Patches where it was, she kissed her goodbye and placed her back in the window. She closed the door and ran downstairs to take care of Cooper. Joanne decided a suitable place for him would be the laundry room. She put a fresh litter box on the floor by the door—along with food and water—patted his head, and closed the door.

When Joanne pulled into the hospital parking lot, Detective Tomkins's unmarked police car and two additional police cruisers were parked near the entrance. She brought her car to a stop in the first parking spot she saw.

In the emergency room, Shae Tomkins waved as she walked up to the triage station.

"Hello. Tom Sherrill was brought in a little bit ago. Is there any way I can find out what his condition is?"

The nurse tapped away on her keyboard for a few moments, looked up from her computer screen, and asked, "Are you family, ma'am?"

Joanne sighed. "No, a friend. I am actually the person who found him on the cellar floor and called 911."

The nurse tapped at her computer and said, "I cannot give out any information unless you are family."

Joanne closed her eyes, shook her head, and began to cry.

Detective Tomkins rushed to Joanne's side, put his arm around her, and looked down at the nurse. "I see your name is Kaytie. May I call you Kaytie?"

The nurse looked up at the detective. "Yes, sir, you may. What can I help you with?"

"When you talk to people, Kaytie, you should look them

in the eyes. It lets them know you are listening to them. It is also a sign of respect. Just a suggestion."

"I am so sorry. I didn't mean any disrespect. It has been a long week."

Shaking his head and smiling, he said, "No problem, Kaytie. We learn something new every day. Let me fill you in on what is going on and who this woman is standing here, in tears, before you. This is Joanne Roberts, the late Adam Peterson's sister and Tom Sherrill's friend. You know Adam, the old fella who volunteered in the children's ward twice a week?"

The nurse nodded. "Yes, I know who you are talking about. He is the most wonderful man, a Korean War vet. The kids adore him. I love listening to the stories he tells the kids about all the planes he flew in the war. What happened to him?"

Shae Tomkins tilted his head a bit to the left and replied, "He is dead, burned 98 percent of his body. On top of that terrible tragedy, Mrs. Roberts finds her good friend Tom Sherrill severely injured on the cellar floor of her dead brother's burned-up house. Then this poor lady rushes into your emergency room and gets the cold shoulder from you—and I witnessed it. Now, what do you think your supervisor, Kathie Tanner, my sister, would think about your behavior? Aren't nurses supposed to have compassion, Kaytie?"

She quickly began tapping on her computer keyboard again. "I have made a note on Mr. Sherrill's admission papers that Ms. Roberts is his sister. She will not have any more problems receiving updates on his condition or speaking with the doctors or nurses. I will see what information I can find out for you now. I will let you know as soon as I have the information. Please take a seat in the waiting room. There is fresh coffee by the vending machine. Please help yourself."

Shae led Joanne to a small couch and helped her take off her coat. "Do you want a cup of coffee, Mrs. Roberts?"

"Yes, that would be super. Two creams, one sugar—and please call me Joanne."

He smiled, gave a courteous nod, and walked away to get the coffee.

Joanne sighed, leaned back on the couch, and closed her eyes. She suddenly sat up straight, her eyes wide with panic. "My God! I have to call Ruby and Bernard!" She reached for her cell phone and gritted her teeth. She knew it was going to be a terribly emotional call.

On the other end of the line, Ruby said, "Sherrill residence."

Joanne took a deep breath. "Hello, Ruby. This is Joanne Roberts. I am going to get right to it. There has been a terrible accident. Tom has been injured. We are at Canyon Heights Memorial, in the emergency room. There has been no report on Tom's condition yet. I arrived about fifteen minutes ago."

Ruby started hyperventilating.

Bernard took the phone and said, "Who is this? What is going on?"

Joanne explained everything.

"We are on our way." Bernard hung up.

A tall, slender man wearing blue scrubs and an unusually bright white lab jacket walked into the emergency room and looked around. "Mrs. Roberts?"

"Yes, right here." Joanne raised up her hand and stood up.

The man walked over to her and held out his hand. "Hello, Mrs. Roberts. I am Dr. Nagy. Tom is alive—but barely. I am sorry to say he is in a coma. He has suffered severe trauma to his head. Tests show he suffered a stroke and had several small seizures. His spleen has been crushed.

He has lost an alarming amount of blood. Tom's blood type is rare, and our supply is limited. We are asking that everyone in the family give blood. One of the nurses will be out shortly to get names and numbers of family members to be contacted. She will take care of contacting everyone on the list. We are moving Tom into surgery now. We expect to be in surgery for at least six hours. There is always a chance there is more damage inside Tom, but we won't know that until we get him into surgery. I will be sure you are updated accordingly. He is fighting like hell. Let's pray he hangs in there and keeps fighting."

Joanne thanked Dr. Nagy, and he hurried off. As she sat down, Shae walked up with two cups of coffee. Joanne let out a long, deflating sigh and began to tell the detective what the doctor had to say about Tom's condition.

Shae cocked his head, tapped his fingers on the side of his cup, and said, "If he walked off the edge of the floor by accident, I would think there would be more damage to his legs. Maybe you missed something the doctor said. I am going to see if I can find out more information." With a crooked eyebrow, Detective Tomkins walked off to investigate.

Moments later, Bernard and Ruby rushed into the emergency room. Ruby had black streaks down her cheeks from her makeup. The look of panic on Bernard's face was enough to make Joanne start crying again. She got up and started over to greet them.

Ruby said, "How is my boy, Joanne? Is he alive?"

Joanne wrapped her arms around Ruby and said, "He's alive, but he is in the fight of his life." She went on to explain the state in which she'd found him and the report she had just received from the doctor.

Bernard sat down, put his head in his hands, and shook

his head. With a trembling voice, he said, "Does anyone know how he fell? I just don't understand how this could happen. Tom is a strong, vigilant man. He knows that farm probably as well as Adam Peterson did. This doesn't sound like a mess he would get himself into. Where is Brenda? Has anyone even called her?"

Joanne put her arm around Bernard and said, "Detective Tomkins was concerned with the injuries Tom had and thought Tom would have injured his legs if he had walked off the edge of the floor. I do not know what his thoughts are in regard to what he feels may have happened since he did not elaborate on his theory. He left me moments before you and Ruby arrived. He went off to see if he could find out more about Tom's condition. He thought I may have misunderstood or missed something the doctor said. I do not believe Brenda has been contacted. I was waiting to see what the doctor said so I had something to report to her. The nurse listed me as Tom's sister so I could get updates on his condition. They wouldn't tell me anything when I arrived, but Detective Tomkins used his influence to be sure I wasn't refused information by the staff."

Bernard put his arm around Joanne. "Stands to reason the person who found our boy should be privy to all information concerning him. Sister it is."

Ruby began pacing the floor and mumbling to herself.

Joanne took her hand and said, "Honey, are you okay?"

Ruby whispered, "Brenda, Brenda, Brenda."

Joanne shook her arm and tried to snap her out of her trance. "I am okay. I will take care of calling Brenda."

Ruby clenched her teeth.

They waited for hours to hear about Tom's surgery.

Joanne looked down at her watch and saw that is was

already a quarter to eight in the evening. "Ruby, don't you think you should call Brenda? She has to be worried."

Ruby had been pacing for hours. She walked over to Joanne and pointed a bony index finger at her. "Don't you worry about when I call that bitch. If it were up to me, I wouldn't let anyone call her. I will call her tomorrow morning. I can't handle dealing with her up here right now. I don't know whether Tom told you or not, but he moved out of their house the day before last. He was contemplating divorce. I always knew she was bad news. My poor Tommy."

Joanne said, "I am so sorry, Ruby. I didn't know. You do what you think is best and let me know if there is anything I can do for you all."

Ruby began pacing again. "Brenda ..."

Bernard hadn't spoken in hours. He was staring out the window by the front entrance.

Joanne took a seat beside him and said, "You okay, Bernard? Is there anything I can get for you? Coffee, water? You all have to be getting hungry. Neither of you will be any use to Tom if you are run down or sick. Let me go get some food for you and Ruby. Okay?"

Bernard walked closer to the window. "I will go see what I can find for us to eat. Would you mind staying here with Ruby? I don't want her left alone. No telling what that woman will do. Anything in particular you would like to eat, Joanne?"

She looked at him with concern and wondered what he meant. "I am happy to sit with Ruby. Anything you get will be fine, Bernard. Thank you so much."

He kissed Ruby on the head. "You stay here, Mama. I am going to get us something to eat. You need to keep your strength up." Bernard hurried down the hall to the cafeteria.

The two women sat in silence for what seemed like hours.

A nurse said, "Sherrill family?"

Ruby got up from her chair. "We are Tom Sherrill's family."

She walked over to the two women. "My name is Ashley. I am Tom's nurse. It is nice to meet you. I am so sorry about Tom and the accident. I assure you we are doing everything possible for him. He is in the best of hands. Tom's surgery went perfectly. There was a quite a bit more soft tissue damage than we expected, so there was obviously more to repair. The surgery went just over eight hours. A craniotomy was performed on Tom to excise the acute subdural hematoma that had formed on the temporal lobe of Tom's brain. He will spend a couple days in intensive care, but he is stable. Dr. Nagy will come out to speak with you shortly. Please have me paged if you have any questions or concerns before the doctor speaks with you."

Ruby shook the nurse's hand. "Thank you for taking the time, young lady."

Ashley nodded and rushed off through the swinging doors.

Ruby paced back and forth and bit her nails. "I suppose we should call Brenda. Let her know her husband is lying in a hospital bed. Not like she will care. But it is the right thing to do. I am going to call her right now and get it over with."

Joanne was watching the television on the wall. A heavyset Mexican man was speaking in Spanish to a group of children who sat on the floor before him. She couldn't understand what he was saying. Joanne went to the front desk. Behind the desk was a large, muscular, blond man who looked like Adonis. His name tag read Allen.

As she began to speak, the young man said, "Hi, ma'am. What may I help you with?"

Joanne felt her face blush, but she welcomed the distraction. "Yes, we are waiting to speak with Tom Sherrill's physician, Dr. Nagy. Will he be available soon?"

Allen looked over the charts on the wall and removed one of the charts from a slot. After looking through the file for a few moments Allen rose from his seat with the file in his hand. "I am going to see what I can find out for you. Please excuse me." Politely nodding, he walked out of the waiting room.

Ruby dialed Tom and Brenda's home number, but there was no answer. She left no message and dialed Brenda's cell number. Again, no answer. "Hi, Brenda. This is Ruby. There has been a terrible accident. Tom has been seriously injured. We are at Canyon Heights Memorial. Come right away." Ruby pressed the red button on her cell phone and paused in thought for a moment. "Oh my God!" With her face full of horror, Ruby ran back into the hospital to find her husband.

Ruby scanned the emergency waiting room, looking frantically for Bernard. She spotted him at the far end of the hallway. He was carrying coffee and snacks.

Joanne noticed the panic in Ruby's eyes and hurried to her side. By the time she reached her, Ruby was hyperventilating again. Joanne ran to the front desk. "Do you all have any of those barf bags back there?"

One of the nurses reached into a cabinet, pulled out a white bag, and handed it to Joanne.

Joanne said, "Here. Put this up to your mouth and take a deep breath." Ruby did as instructed. "That's it, Mama. Breathe in and breathe out."

Bernard took his wife by the hand and helped her over to a sofa.

Ruby pulled the bag away from her face. "I called Brenda, but she didn't answer either phone. I can't stop thinking about Peterson and how he ended up dead. Could Brenda have done this to my boy? Could she have tried to kill my Tommy?"

Joanne and Bernard looked at each other solemnly.

Bernard rubbed her face, "Now, Ruby, don't you go speaking about stuff you don't know nothing about." He looked tired and ready to fall to the ground.

Joanne put her arm around him. "Why don't you take Ruby home, hon? You are both exhausted. Nothing more any of us can do tonight. Neither of you will be any good to your son asleep on your feet."

He let out a sigh and shook his head. "Yeah, I think you have a point, sweet girl. I am gonna take Mrs. Sherrill home. You be sure you get yourself home soon too. Hear me?"

Joanne smiled, hugged him, and said, "I am going to see what the doctor has to say and then get on home to bed. How about we meet back here tomorrow morning at seven?"

Bernard nodded. "You have a deal, darling. See you then."

She kissed him on the cheek and watched as the couple disappeared into the parking lot hand in hand.

As she headed for the coffee machine, a man said, "For Tom Sherrill?"

She rushed over to the gentleman. "Here, I am Tom Sherrill's sister, Joanne Roberts."

"I'm Dr. Nagy." The doctor shook her hand. "Your brother has some very serious injuries. We were able to remove the hematoma on Tom's brain. The clot formed on his temporal lobe, the lobe that controls memory. We know there will be some level of memory loss, but we are unable to know the extent of this loss at this time since he is in a coma. We can't determine the level of memory loss until he wakes up. The fall he sustained had such a force that it crushed part of his frontal lobe. This lobe controls movement and motor skills. The amount of trauma the frontal lobe received was very severe. He had to have fallen directly on his head and with a lot of force. I have never seen a patient survive after this kind damage to the skull and the brain. It is literally a miracle that your brother survived this at all. That young fella has an angel watching over him. Again, we will not know what his physical handicaps are, if any, until he wakes up."

Joanne looked down at her feet and wiped the tears from her eyes. "Is there any way to know when he might wake up?"

The doctor shook his head and said, "I am sorry, Mrs. Roberts. There is no way to know when Tom will wake up. It could be tomorrow, next week, or even next year. We will take each day as it comes and hope he wakes up very soon. Your brother is a strong man. He is a hell of a fighter. He is being transferred to the intensive care unit on the second floor now. He will spend a few days in the ICU—and then he will be admitted onto the rehab floor where he will reside for some time. His stay with us will be long. We are taking good care of him and will monitor your brother very closely. Do you have any more questions for me?"

Joanne shook her head. "Thank you for taking the time to speak with me, Dr. Nagy."

He held out a white business card. "Here is my office number. You can usually have me paged here at the hospital, but please call my office if you need to." He walked away, stopping to flirt with a few of the nurses before he disappeared from sight.

Joanne walked toward the coffee machine, noticing her

reflection in the window as she passed. "Wow, I look like shit." She was embarrassed when the elderly couple to her right looked up at her with disgust. Realizing there was nothing more to do that night, she headed out to her car. She let out a sigh as she drove off into the night.

At home, she wondered whether she should call Ruby and Bernard to update them on Tom's condition. She decided to wait until the morning. There would be plenty of sleepless nights ahead for Ruby and Bernard. Tom's road to recovery was a very long one. *Best to let them rest.* She turned off the lights and went to bed.

The next morning, Joanne awoke to the sound of someone pounding on her front door. She looked at the clock on the nightstand: 7:10. At first, she thought she was dreaming, but she realized it was no dream when she heard the voice. She instantly felt sick to her stomach. She quickly dressed and rushed down to the door.

Brenda held Dillon in her arms. She was extremely tired. Brenda pushed her way past Joanne. "Tom! Tom! Come out, you lying, cheating bastard!" She walked from room to room and called out his name. "He had to be dead—or badly injured—after that fall," she said under her breath.

Brenda knew the spouse was always a suspect at first. With their past and present marital problems, accompanied by her documented mental issues, she was sure she would be at the top of the suspect list. Brenda could make no mistakes—or her crime would be found out. According to the message Ruby left, Tom was at Canyon Heights Memorial, and he was not dead.

"Brenda, calm down. Didn't you get Ruby's message? Tom is in the emergency room at CHM. He has been badly injured. When I arrived to meet him at Peterson's place, I found him on the root cellar floor. The police are ruling it an accident. There will be an official report released to the family, but it appears he fell from the kitchen to the root cellar. He must have slipped off the edge. You would have to see the house to understand."

Brenda turned around and faced Joanne. "So, Tom really is in the hospital?"

Joanne said, "That is what Ruby told you last night. What is wrong with you? You must be out of your mind, Brenda. How dare you barge into my home like this, acting like an insane person? Please leave at once!"

The women stared at each other for a few moments.

"Pardon my intrusion," Brenda said. With a blank stare, she walked toward the front door. She was suddenly quiet and calm. Joanne shook her head as Brenda put Dillon in his car seat, buckled herself in, and drove away.

Joanne shut the door and called Ruby and Bernard.

After three rings, Ruby said, "Sherrill's residence."

"Ruby, it's Joanne. Listen—something very odd just happened here at my house. Brenda was here, and she was out of her mind. I think someone needs to get to the hospital immediately." Her breathing was fast, and she was sweating.

"Calm down, child. What happened?"

Joanne took a deep breath. "I will tell you about it when you and Bernard get to the hospital. It is seven twenty. I will be there by seven forty-five. Tom has been transferred to the ICU on the second floor."

"Okay, dear. We are leaving now. With the way I drive, we will be there by eight twenty if the roads are clear."

Joanne felt a small bit of relief. "See you soon, Ruby. Hurry." She hung up the phone and ran upstairs to get dressed.

At Canyon Heights Memorial, Joanne headed for the elevator. She was a little nervous to see two nuns and a priest also heading for the second floor. An instant wave of hot fear moved through her body. Thoughts and pictures of Tom's dead, cold body flashed over and over in her mind. She began to cry.

The older nun moved toward her and held out a tissue.

Joanne took the tissue and said, "Thank you very much."

The old nun offered a smile and nodded.

The elevator car came to a stop at the second floor. The trio exited the car, and Joanne followed close behind the priest and the nuns. She was relieved when they entered the room of an elderly woman. Joanne could hear a respirator before a nurse closed the door. Joanne lingered for a moment and said a silent prayer for the woman in the bed.

She walked toward the desk and said, "Hi. I am Joanne Roberts, Tom Sherrill's sister. I was told by Dr. Nagy that I would find my brother on this floor this morning. What room is he in please?"

The young man behind the desk looked up at her and ran his fingers through his strawberry-red hair. "Good morning, miss. Your brother is in room 205. Right around the corner. Please sign in when you arrive and when you leave."

She looked at his name tag. "Thank you, Andy. Do

you know if he has had any visitors since he arrived on this floor?"

He picked up the visitor log and turned several pages. "No, Mrs. Roberts. It appears that you are his first visitor."

She was surprised that Brenda had not rushed immediately to the hospital. "Thanks again, Andy. Mr. and Mrs. Sherrill will be along shortly." Joanne gave him a smile and walked toward room 205.

She opened the door and walked into the room. Tom looked pale and small in the hospital bed. There were machines all around him, and he had tubes in his nose and in his arms. She noticed two chairs by the door and moved one of them to his bedside. She sat down and took his hand in hers. His hand was cold; an IV was sticking out of one of the veins on the top of his left hand. Her eyes filled with tears as she kissed his hand. "Oh, Tommy. Please wake up." She stared at him, expecting his eyes to open, but they did not. She was sick to her stomach, thinking about how she might never be able to tell him how she really felt about him. She watched him and waited.

Joanne rose from her chair when she heard Ruby coming down the hall. She walked to the door and walked out to greet them.

When Ruby reached Tom's bedside, she took his hand and kissed his face. Tears fell from her eyes as she whispered, "Tommy, my baby boy, it is Mama. Can you hear me, honey? Son, please. Listen to your mother … wake up."

Bernard placed his arm on her shoulder and pulled her into this chest. They held each other for a few moments before they turned and looked at Joanne.

"What did the doctor have to say last night after we left, dear?" Bernard's eyes were bloodshot with dark circles underneath.

Joanne pulled the other chair to Tom's bedside and asked the couple to sit. She told them what the doctor had said, took the doctor's card from her purse, and handed it to Ruby. "Please put this somewhere safe. If we can't find him at the hospital, the doctor told me we could phone his office. This is the number. He also wrote his personal cell phone number on the back of his business card. I copied both numbers to my cell contacts already."

Ruby placed the card in her wallet.

When Bernard walked out into the hallway, Joanne followed him. She placed her hand on his shoulder and said, "Bernard, we need to talk." He turned around and faced her. His red eyes were full of concern and fear. "Brenda's display at my house this morning was—to say the least—shocking. I was sure I would find her at Tom's side when I got here, but according to the nice young man at the desk, I am the first to visit him. Do you think she could have anything to do with Tom's accident? If you had seen the look in her eyes—she came into my house like Tom was there. It was as if we were having an affair, but if you ask me, she was putting on a show. I swear it was as if she was playing a part like she was trying to cover up for something. She was nervous and sweating. It was not the reaction of a woman concerned about her husband. Why the hell isn't she here?"

Bernard ran his hand over his bald head and closed his eyes. "That damn kid. We told him he needed to call Detective Tomkins. We begged him to call that man and tell him what his crazy wife was up to."

Joanne grabbed his arm and looked him sternly in the eyes. "Bernard, what in the world are you talking about? What has she done? What does Tom know?"

As soon as the last word left her mouth, they heard Brenda coming around the corner.

Bernard took Joanne's hand. "Let's meet at your house later. Ruby and I will tell you what we know. Say nothing to Brenda." He walked quickly back into the room.

Brenda nodded to Joanne as she walked past her and into the room.

Joanne stood quietly outside the room, confused and exhausted. She couldn't decide whether she should go back into the room. Brenda hadn't arrived with the best attitude and hadn't even spoken as she walked by. "That is a plus," she said out loud. Joanne decided it was best to go back into the room and support the family.

As she entered the room, Andy, the ginger-haired nurse, walked in behind her. "Pardon me for the intrusion, everyone. I do need to mention that there are only two visitors allowed per patient in ICU. We have been letting three people in at a time. With that, one of you is going to have to leave. I am afraid four people is too many with all the machines in this small room. Maybe Tom's sister can go for a while. She has been here the longest. I will let you all work that out. Thanks a bunch—and sorry for the inconvenience." He gave a toothy smile and exited the room.

"Sister? Really, Joanne? Sister my ass! I am going to let the front desk know, immediately, that you are impersonating Tom's sister! You're nothing but a whore who can't get her own man." Brenda got up from the chair quickly and walked toward the door.

Bernard grabbed her arm and said, "Listen to me, Brenda. You will do no such thing!" His voice was filled with anger and contempt. "If it weren't for Joanne, our son—your husband—would be dead! You will leave her the hell alone. Do you hear me? Leave her alone! I have had it with your shenanigans. We are very grateful to her. She is allowed to be here. In fact, Detective Tomkins is the person who told the emergency room staff that she was Tom's sister. Maybe Ruby and I ought to go on over and see the good detective. Seems there is plenty we could tell him that I am sure he would be very interested in."

Brenda turned toward Bernard and pulled her arm from his grip. "What exactly do you think you know, old man? Tom would be so hurt to know you are treating me with such disrespect. You should be ashamed of yourself!" She stomped out of the room, mumbling to herself in a dramatic exit.

Joanne looked at Bernard and smiled. "Well, I have had too much excitement already this morning. I need to fill my belly and get some air. Anyone want to have an early lunch? From what I gather, there are some things we need to discuss."

Ruby rose from the chair, kissed Tom on the forehead, and walked out of the room.

"I guess that means yes," Bernard said with a chuckle. "Be back soon, son." He kissed his son's forehead and left the room.

Joanne stood at Tom's side for a moment with her hand on his. "Don't worry, Tommy. We will keep you safe." As she turned to walk away, she swore she heard a noise—like Tom had moved in his bed. Rushing back to his side, she was sad to see Tom was silent and still.

Joanne joined Bernard and Ruby in the parking lot. They decided to have lunch at Joanne's house since the conversation they were about to have required complete privacy. She ordered a large pepperoni pizza and bread sticks from Scotty's Pizza and Subs, which was two blocks from her house.

When Joanne pulled into her driveway, Ruby and Bernard were sitting on the front porch. "I forgot about your lead foot, Ruby!" Joanne called out as she approached the front steps, trying to ease the tension a bit.

Bernard let out a hearty laugh. "Mama is known for that foot!" He kissed his wife softly on her cheek as they followed Joanne into the house.

Patches and Cooper greeted them as they walked through the foyer. "I knew you two would get along famously." She introduced the cats, and for a few moments, they all relaxed and enjoyed each other's company. She took their coats and led them into the living room. "You two have a seat and make yourselves comfortable. Beers all around?"

Ruby nodded. "Yes, dear. I may drink a few. Sure wish I had remembered to stop at the store and pick some up. My brain has been mush for the past couple days."

Joanne hugged her. "I have plenty of beer, Ruby. Let me wait on you for once in your life. How about you, Mr. Sherrill? What will it be?"

He looked at her and sighed. "Do you have anything stronger? Perhaps whiskey?"

With a smile and a wink, she said, "I certainly do! Good old Jim is a pal in these situations." As she turned to leave the room, the doorbell rang. "Pizza's here!"

When Joanne came back into the living room, she was pushing an antique silver serving cart. There was pizza, breadsticks, a large iced tub of beer and a bottle of whiskey. "Adam gave this cart to me last Christmas. We spent a weekend in Amish country. We were in a little shop next to our favorite restaurant. I admired it for quite some time before we left the shop. He went back while I was getting ready for dinner and purchased it. I was so surprised when he rolled it into my living room on Christmas. There was a big red ribbon around it." Her hands moved over the shiny handle as she shared the memory. Wiping a tear from her eye, she said, "Now let's get down to it. What does Tom have on Brenda? Please don't leave anything out. You can be completely honest with me. I will not speak to anyone about what you tell me."

Bernard placed his hand on Ruby's shoulder. "You go ahead and tell her, Mama." Ruby wiped red sauce from her mouth and began reliving the last few weeks. By the time she was finished telling the story, forty-five minutes had passed—and she was in tears.

Joanne's face was flushed, and her brow was sweating. "Is it safe to assume Brenda had something to do with Tom's accident? Don't you two think Detective Tomkins should hear all of this? Why in the hell hasn't someone said something to him already? What else has to happen before someone goes to the police?" She was pacing with a beer in her hand.

Bernard got up from the couch and walked toward the window. "I agree that we need to meet with Detective Tomkins and give him all the information we have, but I would much rather concentrate on Tom for the next week or so before we blow the whistle on that lousy bitch. Once we go to the police, this is going to be all over the news. The media and the cops will make our lives a sick mess. Tom needs our attention and prayers right now." He stared out the window.

Joanne walked over to him, put her arm around him, and said, "I am sorry, Bernard. I am so angry over what happened to Adam, Tom, and little Donnie that I didn't think about anything else. I agree with you. We should wait on speaking with Shae. However, I feel it is important to discuss how long much longer we should keep our silence. I know Donnie was your grandson and Tom is your son, but

Adam was my brother. If Brenda is guilty of these crimes, we need to stop her before she can hurt anyone else."

Ruby joined Joanne and Bernard at the big bay window. "How about we wait until one month from today. By then, Tom will be out of ICU and settled into his rehab routine. God willing, he might be awake. After a month, the three of us will go see Detective Tomkins together. Does that sound acceptable to everyone?"

Bernard and Joanne nodded and said, "Yes."

"That was a nice lunch, Joanne. Thank you so much for having us. Bernard and I are going to go back up to the hospital and then head home. We have been waiting for the weather to break so we can start erecting the greenhouse. We are gonna get some work done on it today. Bernard and I could use an afternoon of distraction. Are you going back to the hospital today?"

Joanne walked them to the door. "I think I am going to stay away for the rest of the day. After Brenda's two meltdowns today, I feel it is wise to distance myself for a day or two. I am in no mood for her shit. She may end up with a fat lip—or worse. I don't want to be someone's prison wife."

Bernard laughed thunderously. "She sure as hell could use a good ass-kicking, honey."

Joanne hugged them both. "Call me in the morning. I will meet you two at the hospital, and we can come back here for some drinks and lunch."

Ruby put her arm around her and kissed her cheek. "I sure wish you were our daughter-in-law, dear. You are such a beautiful, honest, sweet child. Tom adores you--and so do we. I will call you in the morning. Love you."

Joanne watched as they backed out of the driveway.

# TYING UP LOOSE ENDS

Brenda put Dillon down for a nap and walked into the spare room where Tom had been sleeping. She searched the dresser and the closet. She didn't know what she was looking for, but she had to find out what Tom had on her. She couldn't stop thinking about what Bernard said at the hospital. She had to know what they knew and figure out how she was going to deal with them. Brenda searched for over an hour and found nothing. Her anger and fear got the best of her as she picked up a chair and threw it into the full-length mirror on the wall.

She picked up a piece of glass and held it to her wrist for several minutes, shaking and sweating. Staring at herself in what was left of the mirror, she let the piece of glass fall to the floor. Straightening her hair, she calmly walked down the stairs. She knew exactly how to deal with Ruby and Bernard. Brenda removed her address book from the top desk drawer and thumbed to the letter H. "Judy Hammond," she said. Brenda dialed the number, tapped her fingers on the desk, and waited for an answer.

"Hello? Hammond residence."

Brenda's face lit up when she heard Judy's voice on the other end.

Tom and Brenda had met Judy two years earlier at an

ice cream social when she was fourteen. A lovely, blonde girl from a wonderful family, Brenda thought she would be a perfect babysitter for Dillon. Her mother was the principal at Canyon Heights Junior High, and her father was a physician at Canyon Heights Memorial.

She ran into Judy at the grocery store the other day when she was picking up diapers for Dillon. They spoke in depth about Judy babysitting for Dillon on occasion.

"Judy, this is Brenda Sherrill. I am calling to ask if you would be interested in babysitting for Dillon this evening. I have some errands to run after dinner. Are you free tonight— or do you already have plans?"

"Hi, Brenda. I am free tonight, but I don't have a car. Can you pick me up? What time?"

"I will pick you up at five thirty. Will that work for you?" She heard Judy sneeze. "You're not getting a cold, are you, dear? I would hate for Dillon to get sick again. He just got over a cold."

"No, my allergies are acting up. My little brother snuck a stray cat into his bedroom last night. Poor guy was crushed when we found the cat. He can't keep him because of my allergies. He is pretty mad at me right now. Five thirty is good, Brenda. I will see you then."

"Good, Judy—until then." Brenda hung up the phone and skipped out of the room, whistling.

When Bernard and Ruby arrived at Tom's room, there were two doctors and a nurse at his bedside. As they walked toward his bed, they cried out with joy when they saw their son's eyes open. As they rushed to his bed, Dr. Nagy held out his hand for Bernard. "Hello, Mr. and Mrs. Sherrill. We are very excited to see Tom's eyes open. We have not seen any movement—nor has he spoken—but his eyes opening is a wonderful sign. We have run several cognitive tests, and it appears Tom can hear and understands what we say to him. We will run several more tests later today. We want him to sleep for a bit so he can build up his energy. If you two could keep it short, that would be best. You have my number if you have any urgent questions before this afternoon."

Bernard patted Dr. Nagy's shoulder. "Thanks, Doc! We are so happy for any improvement, but this is amazing. God bless you!"

Ruby's eyes filled with tears as she looked down at her son and touched his hand. "What Bernard said, Doc! Thank you very much!"

When the doctors and nurse left the room, Bernard and Ruby sat in silence with Tom for several minutes before they kissed his forehead. Ruby took her son's hand in hers and said, "Rest sweet, good boy." She touched his face and rose from her chair.

"Give 'em hell, Tommy," Bernard said.

Ruby dialed Joanne's cell number as they walked down the hallway, and Bernard put his arm around her. Joanne's phone rang several times with no answer. She left a voice mail and asked her to call when she received the message.

"You should have told the poor child our news, Ruby. You will have her worried to death."

She cocked her head. "She will be fine, dear. As soon as she hears Tom is awake, she will be just fine. We will meet her after our boy gets some rest.

As Joanne turned the shower off, she heard her cell phone ringing. Knowing she would not make it out of the shower and to her phone before the caller was placed into her voicemail, she took her time drying off, wrapped the towel around herself, and went off to see who called. Joanne was intrigued when she saw the missed call was from Ruby. She dialed Ruby's cell right away.

"Hello, dear! We have wonderful news! Tom is awake!"

Joanne's eyes began to fill with tears. "Oh, thank you, sweet Lord!" The tears streamed down her face.

"It is so wonderful! Our boy is awake. We only saw him for a few minutes since the doctor asked us to keep our visit brief. They are running more tests this afternoon, but Dr. Nagy said Tom can hear. He is aware and alert. We are heading to the mall to kill some time while Tommy naps. We will meet you at the hospital at three. Does that sound okay?"

Joanne wiped the tears from her eyes. "I will see you two crazy kids then." She ended the call and set the phone on her dresser.

The trio had a brief visit with Tom. There was no change, but his eyes were still open. They could tell he recognized them when they entered his room.

What joy it brought to them to see his boyish face and blue eyes.

They chatted for about twenty minutes and then decided to let the patient rest.

Bernard followed behind the two women, listening, as they made plans to meet at Tom's room the following afternoon. "We have breakfast every Sunday morning with George at seven thirty and then it is on to Mass at eleven. We should be here at two o'clock tomorrow afternoon, Joanne, weather permitting. Does that suit your schedule, sweet girl?" Ruby touched Joanne's face lovingly.

"Of course, Ruby—and please let me take you both to lunch after our visit." Joanne felt as though she had to take care of Tom's parents in his absence.

"We will be here with bells on!" Ruby exclaimed with a wink.

They all embraced and said their goodbyes.

Bernard and Ruby sat in silence on the ride home, both smiling from ear to ear.

As Bernard pulled into the driveway, it began to snow. "Oh, Mama, I don't know about working on the greenhouse tonight with it getting dark outside and the snow beginning to fall."

Ruby looked out the window and said, "Oh, I don't know about that, Daddy. The snow isn't gonna hurt you none. We can set up some of those spotlights you and the boys use when you get to working on your trucks into the late hours. It will be fun, baby, and it will take our minds off of the dark cloud hanging over our heads. I promise. I will make some hot cocktails and light the barrels."

He put his hand on her leg and rubbed her gently. "Okay, Mama. It is a date!" He brought the truck to a stop and rushed to the passenger side, opening the door for his wife. "Come on. Hurry up, old lady. It is already quarter to six, and we've got lots to do." He pinched her butt as they walked up the stairs.

Brenda looked at her speedometer as she raced through town to pick up Judy. Just as she applied the brake, she saw the lights and heard the siren. "Fuck!" Brenda shouted as she pulled over to the side of the road. She waited for the police officer to approach her window, nervously tapping on the steering wheel. Looking in her rearview mirror, Brenda could see the car that pulled her over was not the normal black and white police car. This car was all black, and the lights were mounted on the dashboard. She looked over her shoulder as Detective Shae Tomkins walked slowly toward her. She thought it was strange that a detective would pull her over for speeding.

"Good evening, Brenda. I was leaving the station, going home, when you ran a red light—right in front of me. I was compelled to pursue and imagine my surprise to find you and Dillon racing through town, running lights. Is everything okay?" He laughed genuinely and cocked his head to the side.

"I am so sorry, Detective Tomkins. I am late picking up Dillon's babysitter, and I was rushing. I am so sorry. With everything that has been going on lately, I am afraid my mind is in so many places. I wasn't paying attention to my driving in the manner that I should. I am so sorry for driving unsafely. Are you going to give me a ticket?"

Shae scratched his head for a few moments. "I am going to give you a break this time, Brenda. I already ran your license plate. You have no prior violations. You have a spotless record. Please slow down and obey all the traffic laws. Oh, and one more thing. Funny that I have run into you because I have been meaning to get in contact with you. I have some questions for you in regard to Tom's accident. Can you call me on Monday morning and set up a time to come in?"

"I don't know what I can tell you about his accident, Officer. I wasn't there."

He turned to walk toward his car. "Give me a ring anyway please—and we will set up that time. I have a few standard questions before I can close the file and stamp it *accidental*. Our talk should only take a few minutes of your time."

Brenda smiled at the detective. "I will talk to you tomorrow, Officer. Have a nice evening." As he drove into traffic, she signaled her way onto the busy road and drove on.

Finally arriving at Judy's house, 555 Sherman Drive, Brenda could see the girl walking out her front door and waving to her. She returned the gesture to the teenager and waited for her to get into the car. "Hello, Judy. So nice to see you again. Sorry I am late. Dillon has been ornery and fussy today. I think he is cutting a few teeth. He ate a wonderful dinner and is tired. I am sure he will be ready to go down for the night when we get back to the house."

Judy fastened her seat belt as Brenda pulled out of the driveway.

Once inside the house, Brenda showed Judy around. Glancing at her watch, Brenda said, "It is already six o'clock. Where is the evening getting to? Dillon is ready for bed. Let's go put him down, and I will get out of your hair."

Judy laughed, and the two went off to put the boy to sleep for the night.

"Piece of cake! He is such an agreeable baby." Brenda was grinning from ear to ear as they closed the door to the nursery. She picked up her purse and keys, hurrying toward the door. "Thanks, Judy. I don't know what time I will be home. If it is late and you are tired, please feel free to sleep on the couch. I will take you home in the morning after I make us both some eggs and bacon. You have my cell number, and the emergency contact numbers are on the fridge. Don't hesitate to call me."

"Everything will be fine, Brenda. See ya later." Judy closed and locked the door behind her.

Brenda zipped up her jacket as she hurried to her car.

It was dark, and the temperature was dropping quickly. She hopped into her car at six fifteen, took a deep breath, pressed hard on the gas pedal, and tightened her grip on the steering wheel. She was eager to have a chat with her in-laws. Glancing out the window, she noticed the snow had begun to fall again.

As Brenda signaled onto old Route 20, her mind was racing. So much had happened that she didn't anticipate. She had decided to go with the moment and let nature take its course. She didn't know what she would say to them or how she would get them to share what they knew about the past day's events, but she was determined to take care of the situation for good. "No more shit from those two fucks," she said as she pressed harder on her accelerator. "Nobody is going to separate my Dillon and me." The look on her face was stern, and her brow had begun to sweat. She pressed on as the snow turned into a blizzard.

Brenda turned down Stanford Way, where the farm had belonged to the Sherrill family two hundred years. Bernard grew up there, and so had his father before him. She always loved her visits to the farm, feeling its history in every piece of wood and block in the beautiful house. She felt sad for a moment, knowing she would never again sit at the long, rustic table and share a meal with the family again. The laughter and love she experienced at that table was nothing like the experiences with her own parents at their cold, dismal table.

Before turning onto the long driveway, she stopped the car and looked into the rearview mirror. "Don't worry, Dillon. Mommy will make sure we have that kind of love and togetherness with our family one day. I promise you, sweet boy." She was surprised to see her reflection fade into her son's face. She closed her eyes, opened them, and saw her own face staring back at her. For a brief moment, she did not like what she saw—but the feeling left as soon as it had come.

About halfway up the driveway, there was a small turnoff where she would park and walk the rest of the way. She didn't want Bernard and Ruby to see her coming.

The snow was coming down so hard that she couldn't see five feet in front of her. She slipped on a patch of ice and fell to her knees. She immediately felt a warm sensation that she recognized. Blood was gushing from a gash on her palm. She started to panic as she searched for something to bandage her hand with. She was wearing one of Tom's old flannels and ripped off a piece that was big enough to wrap around her hand. She quickly wrapped her hand, tied a small knot to secure the wrap, and hurried up the driveway.

As Brenda approached the house, she heard Bernard's new excavator. She walked around the left side of the house and saw Bernard removing buckets of frozen soil with the machine. She giggled. *What is that crazy old asshole doing out in this shitty weather?* Ruby appeared with two large coffee cups. Brenda was close enough to see the steam rising from the cups.

Ruby hopped up on the machine, handed the cup to her husband, kissed his forehead, and sat on his lap. Bernard turned off the machine, and they chatted for a few minutes. Bernard pinched Ruby's large breast, and she climbed down. As Ruby headed back to the house, she shook her head and laughed.

Brenda felt a wave of regret to have to do to Ruby what she knew she must.

As Ruby disappeared into the house, Brenda followed her. Better to deal with her mother-in-law first since the machine would drown her cries. Just as Brenda turned to follow Ruby, Bernard got off the excavator, grabbed a shovel, and began to chip away at the frozen ground and roots that were stuck in the teeth of the bucket. Without thinking, Brenda ran and jumped onto the machine. She released the clutch, stepped on the gas, and ran over Bernard. The engine stalled as he let out a bloodcurdling cry.

The screen door on the wraparound porch swung open, and Ruby ran outside. Brenda ducked behind the barn and hid in the blanket of heavy, falling snow.

Ruby reached her love and saw that he was dead. She shouted and cursed at God. She fell to her knees and then to the ground, clutching her chest.

For at least fifteen minutes, Brenda watched her in-laws on the ground. There was no movement. Freezing and trembling from the cold, Brenda decided it was time to check out her handiwork. As she neared the two downed lovers, the smell of metal was so strong in the air that she gagged, almost vomiting at the smell of blood and what she had done to Bernard. She stopped for a moment, standing silent in thought, and stared down at Bernard's mangled body. "Sorry, old fella. At least it was quick. I am a little disappointed I didn't get a chance to play rough with your wife. What a bonus that old hag dropped dead! I think this worked out for the best, Pops, because I think that mean, weathered old witch would have beat my skinny white ass! What do you think, Mr. Sherrill? Oh, sorry, you can't speak– because you're fucking dead!" She never noticed she was standing in a pool of blood that was flowing from Bernard's body.

With an evil shrill, laughing hysterically, Brenda walked

back toward the house, leaving size-six bloody footprints. The footprints disappeared from sight as she drew closer to the porch, the snow cleansing the blood from the bottom of the hiking boots Tom had bought her a month ago for her birthday. It was Brenda and Tom's tradition to give presents to each on their birthdays. She had given him a Zippo lighter for his collection that day. It was a twenty-four-carat lighter that Brenda had inscribed with one word: "Forever."

As she began to climb the steps to the porch, it stopped snowing. She never noticed the footprints behind her or the blood splatter on the side of her boot. The snow had not hidden her last few steps.

Once inside the house, Brenda realized she had blood on the left side of her neck. "How did I get this shit on me?"

On her way to the kitchen to wash her hands, she stopped to view the family pictures that were neatly hung on the living room wall. She sighed and took down a picture that was nestled in a silver frame. It was the Sherrill family photo they had been taking every three years, on New Year's Eve, as long as the tight-knit family existed. It was one of the most important and exciting traditions the family shared. Preparing for the photo was a huge affair.

Every member of the family was asked to suggest where the picture should be taken, what the family should wear, and even how the family members should be seated and positioned. There was a big meal and celebration that followed the festive, cherished event. It took months to plan since the family was a large and opinionated. After many discussions, they always ended up agreeing on a spectacular event. This particular family photo was taken the weekend after Brenda and Tom lost their baby. They had both shown up for the pictures, but the hurt and grief in their hearts showed on their faces. They declined the copy offered to them by Bernard and Ruby. It was too hard for them to look at the picture without Brenda's baby bump.

Smiling warmly, Brenda said, "I know just what to do with this."

After cleaning the sink and getting rid of the blood, Brenda dried her hands, zipped her coat, and walked out to her car. Before she opened the door, she took in one last deep breath of the beautiful land. Looking up at the star-filled sky, she said, "Good riddance." She breathed a sigh of relief, got into her car, and drove back to Canyon Heights.

She was relieved that Judy was still awake, watching reruns of *I Love Lucy*. She sat with her for a while and asked how Dillon had done while she was away. Judy's report was pleasing to Brenda, and she decided the evening was a complete success.

With midnight approaching, Judy politely announced it was time for her to get home since she attended early Mass with her family and wanted to be well rested. Brenda collected Dillon and bundled him up to take Judy home.

Once they arrived at the Hammond home, Brenda walked Judy to her front door and handed her three fifty-dollar bills.

Judy's eyes widened. "Brenda, this is too much money. You must have given me the wrong bills." Brenda looked at Judy with an innocent grin. "No, dear. It is the right amount. This is a most joyous night, and you earned it, Judy."

She looked at Brenda and said, "What happened to your shirt? It is torn and looks like there is blood on it. Did you cut yourself?"

Brenda replied nervously, "This is one of Tom's old shirts. I wear it when I paint. I got it stuck in the car door. I will mend it tomorrow."

They said their goodbyes, and Brenda headed home, feeling confident that she had taken care of her problem that night. She was wrong.

# GONE

George McClure's 150 acres has been in his family for more than two hundred years. The McClures and Sherrills had always been family. When George's wife died five years earlier, he didn't think he would survive the loss of his one and only love, but Bernard and Ruby never left his side. Weeks after the loss of Mary, Ruby invited George for breakfast before Sunday Mass, and it has been a weekly tradition ever since.

George awoke early that Sunday morning to his rooster crowing at four o'clock, earlier than usual. "Damn rooster. I should eat him," he said with a laugh as he crawled out of bed.

Dressed and ready for the cold, George went out to the barn to give the cows a quick milking. By seven o'clock, he headed back to the house to clean up for breakfast.

He had an odd feeling in his gut since he awoke, but he couldn't put his finger on it. "Something ain't right this morning," he said. Grabbing the fresh gallon of milk, he put on his coat and headed across the street for the meal he waited for all week.

Halfway up the driveway, he noticed something red on the ground—near a set of tire tracks that were barely visible through the snow—and walked over to investigate. Kneeling down, he touched the red substance and broke the top crust of ice. He put his fingers to his nose and inhaled deeply. The smell was faint, but he realized it was blood. Just to the right of the partially frozen puddle, a tree root was covered in blood. Large drops led away from it. "What in the hell?"

The suspicious feeling crept back into his belly as he proceeded up the driveway.

The front door was open.

"Good morning, Sherrills! Are you trying to freeze yourselves to death on this cold Sunday morning?"

No answer.

He headed to the kitchen to greet his friends. He smelled no coffee brewing or biscuits baking in the oven. As he entered the kitchen, he was shocked to find it cold and dark. Alarmed and filled with worry, he headed out toward the barn. In the distance, he saw an object on the ground next to Bernard's new excavator. He ran toward the machine. George spotted Ruby first and fell to the ground. "No. No!" He pulled her into his arms and cradled her lifeless body as tears fell from his eyes. He saw Bernard's mangled body under the machine and began to scream. George buried his head in Ruby's neck and wept uncontrollably for many minutes. He left her body on the ground where he found her, rose to his feet, and walked back to the house to call the police.

Within thirty minutes, the farm that was once filled with laughter and joy was filled with police cars, ambulances, and the coroner's van.

George sat on the porch with his head in his hands. Tears streamed down his cheeks. Two police officers sat beside him, writing down every word he said. The officers finished their questioning just in time for George to see his dear friends wheeled past him covered in white sheets.

With sadness in his heart and his head hung low, George stood up and walked home. Once he reached the steps to his porch, he looked up and saw the swing Bernard and Ruby had made him for his seventy-fifth birthday. He looked at it for a few moments and rubbed the beautiful oak planks. He was happy for a moment, remembering how he had come home that evening and wondered what the bright pink thing was on his porch. It seemed to be floating and ghostlike. Ruby had covered it with a pink sheet. He giggled at the memory of how he had walked up the steps and looked at the strange, colorful sheet. When Ruby and Bernard had jumped out and shouted "Happy birthday, you old bastard," he had almost peed his pants. The three old friends had laughed and laughed at his reaction.

"Oh my god! What will I do without the two of you?" George sobbed and ran his fingers through his white hair. Lost in thought, he didn't notice the man walking up the sidewalk.

"Mr. McClure?"

No answer.

"Mr. McClure, I am Detective Joseph Scarth. Are you okay?"

George raised his head, his eyes red and swollen. "I am George McClure. What can I do for you?" He wiped his eyes with his shirt.

"I am wondering if you are up for a few questions sir. Better yet, would you agree to going across the road to the Sherrill property and walking me through what you found today?"

Joseph Scarth was the youngest detective, at twenty-five, in the history of the Jackson Police Department. He was a retired, decorated sergeant major who had served four tours in Iraq without losing a single soldier.

As the men walked across the road, Detective Scarth watched George closely. The young cop had already walked the crime scene and was aware of the bloody drops and root next to the tire tracks.

George paused at the turnout and stared at the blood.

Joseph asked, "What do you see, George?" There was a long silence as George stared at the blood on the ground.

"Have you ever seen something like this, George?" Detective Scarth pointed at the blood and waited for the old man's response.

"I don't remember seeing anything like this on the Sherrill's property ever." George began to sob uncontrollably.

The detective took George by the arm, and they proceeded up the driveway.

In the house, Detective Scarth asked George to lead him through his earlier findings. The tale was hard on him, but he relived the horrid ordeal with Joseph. Standing outside by the excavator, both men could hear the telephone ringing over and over again. "Maybe we should answer it," George said, wiping his eyes with the sleeve of his flannel coat.

They walked back to the house as the ringing continued.

In the kitchen, George said, "Can I interest you in some coffee, Detective? Ruby was a simple woman, but she spared no expense with her coffee. She always had the best around. I could sure use a cup. You game, sir?"

The phone was still ringing.

Detective Scarth said, "Yes, please. I would love a cup of the good stuff. That is, if you don't mind making it." He picked up the phone. "Hello? Sherrill's residence." He could hear noise in the background. "Hello? Sherrill's residence."

Joanne said, "May I please speak with Ruby or Bernard?"

Detective Scarth said, "May I ask who is calling?" As

a young detective, Joseph did not have much experience delivering bad news.

"My name is Joanne Roberts. I am a good friend of the Sherrill family. Ruby and Bernard were supposed to meet me at the hospital at two o'clock this afternoon. It is now three fifteen, and they haven't arrived. Where are they?"

"I am sorry to be the one to tell you this, Mrs. Roberts, but Ruby and Bernard were found deceased early this morning."

Joanne said, "There must be some mistake! Please tell me this isn't true!"

George took the phone from the detective and put it to his ear. "Joanne, this is George McClure. I am so sorry, sweetheart, but it is true. I found them this morning when I came over for our weekly breakfast."

Joanne began to cry.

Joseph took the phone from George and said, "Joanne, do you think you are okay to drive out here to have a talk with me? Maybe you can shed some light on a few things that aren't adding up."

There was a short silence.

"Yes, Officer. I can be there in an hour. Is that acceptable?"

"Yes, that is perfect, Mrs. Roberts—and please call me Joseph."

"Okay, I will see you in a little bit. Please ask George to stay with you until I get there. I have some questions for him, and I don't think he should be alone right now. And please call me Joanne."

"Okay, Joanne. We will be waiting for you. Drive safe."

Joanne wanted to see Tom before she got on the road. As she entered the room, Tom's blue eyes opened. She sat beside his bed and placed her hand on his. Looking into

Tom's beautiful eyes, she thought about how sad Tom would be when he found out about his parents. She looked away and wiped a tear from her cheek.

Tom whispered, "Joanne."

She jumped from her seat and ran to the door. "Come quick. Tom is awake!"

Suddenly, the room was full of chaos.

"Dr. Nagy, please report to room 205 immediately."

Joanne stood in the doorway as the nurses hooked Tom up to machines.

Dr. Nagy appeared at the end of the hall and rushed toward her. His white lab coat looked like Batman's cape as he ran down the hall. He took her by the hand. "Mrs. Roberts, what did Tom say to you? What were you doing when he spoke?"

Joanne removed a tissue from her purse, wiped a tear from her eye, and said, "I was holding his hand, and he said my name."

Dr. Nagy let go of her hand and said, "Please give us some time with him, Mrs. Roberts. I will call you with an update in a few hours." Before she could say anything, he rushed into the room, shutting the door behind him.

She walked down the hallway to the nurse's station, but she didn't recognize any of the faces behind the counter.

"Can I help you, miss?" the young woman behind the desk said with a smile.

Joanne looked at the young nurse's name tag. "Yes, Sheryll. I need to talk to someone about the patient in room 205."

Sheryll rose from her chair. "Of course, dear. You can speak to me. What can I do for you?"

Joanne paused for a moment. She couldn't believe the words that were about to come out of her mouth. "Thank you, Sheryll. I need to inform Dr. Nagy about something, but I didn't get the chance to tell him before he went into Tom's room."

The pretty, brown-haired nurse came around the counter with a clipboard and said, "What would you like Dr. Nagy to know?"

Joanne dropped her purse and began to cry.

Sheryll bent down, picked up the purse, and handed it to Joanne. "Honey, why are you crying? Your brother is awake and talking. What is the problem?"

Joanne said, "I just spoke with a police officer in Jackson. He informed me that our parents were found dead this morning. I want to be sure my brother does not watch the television in his room—in case it is mentioned on the news. I am concerned such news will hinder Tom's recovery." Joanne had almost forgot the detective's lie.

"I am so sorry to hear this, Mrs. Roberts! Your poor family is suffering so much! Please accept my sincere condolences! I will be sure to inform Dr. Nagy about your parents' unfortunate passing. I am sure Dr. Nagy will agree with you." Sheryll took Joanne's hand. "Is there anything I can do for you, dear?"

Joanne wiped her face and said, "Thank you, Sheryll, but I don't think there is anything else you can do right now except inform the doctor of our loss. I am heading to Jackson right now to talk to the detective. Please have Dr. Nagy call me once he has examined my brother."

Sheryll hugged Joanne, assuring her she would take care of informing the doctor.

"Thank you, Sheryll. I am pleased and comforted to know my brother is in good hands. She turned and hurried toward the elevator.

The drive to Jackson seemed like days. Joanne was

waiting to wake up from the nightmare. Arriving at the long driveway that led to the farm, she knew it was no nightmare. It was real life. She proceeded up the drive, pausing as she passed the red snow. "What the fuck is that?" She got out of her car and kneeled beside the red substance. Tears began to fall from her eyes. "Brenda, that fucking bitch!" Joanne got back in her car and drove the rest of the way in tears.

At the end of the driveway, a tall man walked out of the house and waited for her on the porch.

Joanne put the car in the park and got out.

The man walked down the steps. "Joanne?" He held out his hand to greet her.

She walked toward the man who. "Yes, I am Joanne. Detective Joseph Scarth?"

"Yes, but, again, please call me Joseph. We can dispense with formalities. I am very sorry for your loss."

Joanne's head hung low as they entered the house.

George rose from his chair, hurried toward her, and wrapped his arms around her.

They both sobbed uncontrollably.

Joanne gently pulled away from the sad embrace. "George! Oh my God, George. What in the hell is happening?"

The old man took her by the arm and guided her to a chair near the door. "Honey, please sit. You need to be sitting for this." Slowly, with water flowing steadily from his eyes, George told the horrible tale from his first waking moment that fateful Sunday to the very point they were all at now.

Detective Scarth scribbled furiously in his notepad, and Joanne planted her head in her hands and cried.

When George finished, Joanne stood up and said, "Brenda! She did this! Oh my God. We could have stopped this! First Donnie, then Petersen, Tom, now Ruby and Bernard! Oh my God! What have we done?"

The detective looked up from his notebook. "Wait a minute, Joanne. Slow down. What are you talking about? Who is Brenda? What do you mean?"

Joanne sat down in the chair, and George put his hand on her knee. "Dear, please tell the good detective and myself what you are sorry for. I don't know about the detective, but I am very confused. Not because I am an ancient, fucking old, sad man, but because you are speaking in riddles. Please, child, get a hold of yourself and tell us what in the hell you are talking about!"

Joanne let out a long sigh, wiped her eyes, and began to tell the horrific tale. Joanne explained to Scarth that Brenda was Tom's wife, formerly Brenda Miller of New Berry Falls, the snotty daughter of Mayor Michael and Fiona Miller. She continued with the death of Donnie, explaining how Brenda's scarf ended up in Donnie's crib, the pillow on the floor that shouldn't have been there, and how Brenda took off with Dillon. She spoke of the fire that took Petersen's life and how she had found Tom in the root cellar of the old vet's farm house.

Once again, there was silence in the room.

Joseph said, "Joanne, let me get this straight. Brenda is Tom's crazy wife, she killed one of her newly adopted twins, then Tom confided in his best friend Adam Petersen, she found out, killed him, then to silence Tom, she pushed him into Petersen's root cellar, and thought she killed him. To her surprise, the poor son of a bitch lived. Thinking he had confided in his parents, she murders both of them to silence them? Really?" The detective was pacing the floor and shaking his head.

Joanne cried out, "Yes, all of it—yes!"

The two men looked at each other for several moments. George threw his coffee mug at the fireplace. "Jesus Christ! That fucking crazy bitch! Ruby has been ranting about her for years! She never trusted her or bought her prim and proper attitude. She was right all this time, and you kids kept this to yourselves? I never thought much about her babble, dismissing it as a mother's jealousy. Holy shit. The old broad was right all these years!"

Holding his hands high above his head, Detective Scarth shouted, "Both of you, stop this right now. Sit the hell down and think about what you are saying!"

Joanne and George sat down as instructed.

Detective Scarth said, "Okay, let's just say, for one moment, you two have this all figured out—and Brenda is guilty of all you say she is. You can't go around pointing the finger at the mayor's daughter! It is not procedure or how things are done! If there is any truth to what you two are saying, we have to be very careful in how we proceed." Joseph ran both hands through his hair, turned around, and froze. His eyes were fixed on the family photo wall. He walked toward the wall and noticed a spot where the photograph was missing. He removed the picture to the left and saw the dark border on the white wall as if that photo had been there for many years. He compared it to the spot to the right of the photograph, and there was no border. "Do either of you know what photograph was here and where it could have gone? Did the Sherrills remove it recently?"

George said, "May we get out of our chairs and look, sir?"

The detective chuckled. "Yes, George. Will you both get up and look?"

The two of them walked over the wall.

Joanne said, "I am sad to say I haven't been in this house

since their last Christmas party, two years ago, and I don't remember any photograph in that spot."

George said, "Well, I have been here every Sunday for the last several years—and a regular pop-in Pete during the week. I do know what picture was hanging there. It was the family photo. They took a family picture every three years—on New Year's Eve. Take a look at all those family photos taken. The photo that is missing was taken just this past New Year's Eve. I know damn well that picture was hanging there last Sunday because Ruby made a joke about cutting Brenda's face out of it—or maybe even drawing a mustache on her. Bernard snapped at her and insisted that she leave the photograph where it hung and exactly as it was. He made her promise that she would not alter it or remove it. The good, honest woman she was, Ruby promised him and sealed the deal with a slap on his backside." George laughed as he relived the fond memory.

Joseph took out his notebook and began writing in it. "Okay, now we are getting somewhere. I want the two of you to go home now—and do not speak of anything you have seen or heard here tonight. If Brenda is responsible and learns of anything we have discussed here tonight, you may both be in danger. The two of you are the only witnesses at this point, besides Tom, and he is no good to us in the condition he is in. I don't want either of you to breathe a word of this to anyone. If you keep a journal, don't write it down or even think about it. For now, put it in a safe place deep inside your heads." He reached in his jacket and pulled out two business cards. "If either of you think of anything else, call me right away. In the meantime, I am going to contact the Canyon Heights Police Department, set up a meeting with the lead detective who investigated the death of Adam Petersen, and compare some notes. Again, I have to stress to not mention that we had this meeting to anyone. Do you both understand?"

Joanne and George nodded.

Joseph handed Joanne a piece of paper and asked her to write down all of her contact information. She did as she was asked and handed the paper back to Joseph.

Joseph said, "Mr. McClure, I have all of your information recorded already. You and I are square for now."

Joanne stood up and extended her hand to Joseph. "Thank you for listening. I hope you can get all of those affected by the recent tragedies justice and closure. I will be in touch with you if you don't contact me first. Now, if you fine gentleman will excuse me, I need to head back to Canyon Heights. It is getting late, and I am exhausted. I want to get up to the hospital to check on Tommy first thing in the morning." She put on her coat, looked around the house, hugged George, wiped a tear from her eye, and headed out the door.

George said, "You listen here, young fella. You do the right thing and ride this mess out until you put that hateful bitch behind bars or in the ground. Do *you* understand?"

Detective Scarth nodded and said, "I give you the oath of a soldier and a police officer. I will be sure justice is served, my friend." He patted George on the back and walked him to the door.

The tired old man, once again alone, walked out the door and down the steps.

Joseph watched until he disappeared from sight. The detective walked to the family wall and stared at it for several minutes. "What in the fuck happened here last night?" He turned off the light, walked out the door, and locked it behind him. He felt a cold chill go through his body as he walked down the front stairs. He knew, in his gut, that Joanne and George were right—and he began to fear for their safety.

# COLLABORATING DETECTIVES

The next morning, it was business as usual for Detective Shae Tomkins. He stopped at the Ramos family's bakery just as he had every workday for the past seven years. The bakery was the oldest business in Canyon Heights and was famous for their French roast coffee and apple fritters, which were made fresh daily. He treated himself once a week to the sweet treat, and today was the day he would taste the apple-cinnamon goodness he looked forward to.

Martina Ramos, the youngest of four daughters, greeted him as he walked through the door. She gave him a wink and went to the kitchen to bring him out a fresh, warm fritter. The detective removed the lid from his coffee mug and inhaled the fragrance from the fresh-brewed coffee as he poured it into his cup.

Glancing around the shop, he noticed the same old-timers sitting around the same table, talking like they did every morning. Their usual conversations consisted of "the War," John Wayne, and how fat and mean all their wives had grown over the years. As he listened to them, he realized the topic of their conversation was quite different than all the other mornings. With each word they spoke, his heart sank more. "Ruby and Bernard Sherrill were found yesterday morning—tragically killed on their farm in Jackson." Shae walked over to the newspaper machine, put in two quarters, and removed a copy of the Canyon Heights *Chronicle*. When he saw the cover of the newspaper, he dropped his coffee cup. It hit the floor with a loud thud, spilling black liquid all over the tile.

The men looked over at him and one said, "Officer, are you all right? Do you need a hand?"

Shae grabbed a towel from the counter and bent down to clean up the mess at his feet. He hadn't heard the man offer his help. The elderly gentleman walked over to where the detective was frantically cleaning up the mess. "Shae, what has got you spooked? I can see by the look on your face that you are upset. Talk to me, young fella!"

Detective Tomkins got to his feet, shook his head with disbelief, and said, "The Sherrills? I was just with them. Their son was seriously injured at Adam Petersen's property a few days after the old vet lost his life in the fire that destroyed his farm—and now Tom is over at Canyon Heights Memorial in a coma. I am so saddened for the Sherrill family. And to top it all off, Tom and his wife buried one of the twins they just adopted. That poor family has suffered so much. Life can be so unfair."

The man patted Shae on the back. "Sonny, if you live as long we have, unfortunately, you will probably endure much more, especially in your line of work."

Detective Tomkins picked up his coffee cup, hurried to the door, and said, "Sir, please thank Martina and tell her something has come up. I have to get to the police department right away." Before the old man could answer, Shae disappeared was out the door.

The detective's thoughts drifted to the previous Saturday evening when he had witnessed Brenda speeding through town and running the red light. She seemed agitated, and the sweat on her brow didn't belong there with the snow falling outside. He couldn't get the picture of her out of his head. *There was something in her eyes.* Shae pushed the accelerator to the floor.

At the police station, Shae hurried into his office, ignoring the "good morning" greetings from the other officers and the secretary at the front desk. He immediately noticed the red light blinking on his desk phone, alerting him that he had a voice mail. Detective Tomkins picked up the phone, entered his password, and listened to the single voicemail. It was Detective Joseph Scarth from the Jackson Police Department. The message was brief and to the point, simply requesting that he call the Jackson PD detective as soon as he received the voice mail. Joseph left his office and cell number. "The matter is of great urgency." Shae dialed Joseph's office number.

"Detective Scarth here, how may I help you?"

Clearing his throat, Shae replied, "Good morning, Detective. This is Detective Shae Tomkins. I just received your message. What can I do for you?"

Grabbing his notebook, Joseph said, "Good morning to you as well. By any chance, have you seen the newspaper or listened to the news this morning about the tragedy that occurred sometime Saturday evening, here in Jackson, out at Ruby and Bernard Sherrill's farm? I believe we may have a common interest in the events that transpired. Do either of the names Joanne Roberts or George McClure ring a bell to you?"

Tapping the desk with his fingers, Shae said, "Yes, I overheard some of the locals speaking about the Sherrills this morning when I stopped for coffee. I also read the article in the *Chronicle*. I had the pleasure of spending some time with Ruby and Bernard in the past few days. They were honest, good people. I was shocked and saddened to hear of their passing. And, yes, sir, I am acquainted with Mrs. Roberts. Why do you ask? What is this about?"

Joseph sat up in his chair and said, "Detective Tomkins, I would rather speak with you in person in regard to this matter. Would it be okay with you if I come to your office later this morning … say around eleven?"

Shae looked at the clock and his schedule for the day. It was seven thirty, and he was meeting with the lead fire investigator over at the Petersen farm at eight. He had no appointments after that. "Can we make it noon? I have to be somewhere at eight, and I don't know for sure how long it will take. Does noon work for you?"

There was a pause on the other end. "Noon works just fine. I will see you then."

The two said goodbye, and the call ended.

Shae sat back in his chair and stared at the wall. *There was something about her eyes.*

When Detective Tomkins arrived at the Petersen farm, Lieutenant Nicholas Myers was already hard at work. As Shae approached what was left of the farm, he took note of the yellow, crime scene tape that had been placed around the large propane tank near the old shed, about fifty yards from the back porch.

Lieutenant Myers walked over and said, "Good morning, Detective."

They shook hands.

"Morning, Lieutenant Myers. Unfortunately, I can't say

it is all that *good*. What a sad, tragic accident this is, wouldn't you say?"

Nicholas took off his hat, scratched his head, and said, "Indeed it is, Shae, but *accident?* Well, I am not so sure about that. Come over here and take a look at this." The investigator walked toward the propane tank and motioned for Shae to follow.

Lieutenant Myers knelt beside the propane tank, moved the yellow tape aside, and pointed to the spot on the propane tank where the valve should've been. "Here is where the valve is located on these industrial-sized propane tanks—and there is the valve." The lieutenant pointed to the ground on the side of the tank.

"And what about the other two tanks on the property?" Detective Tomkins asked, kneeling beside the investigator.

Rising to his feet, Lieutenant Myers replied, "They are all in the same condition—with the valve on the ground next to the tank. I found an old pipe wrench out near the third propane tank on the west bank of the pond. Walking the grid around the crime scene, I tripped over it. I bagged it and put it in the van. I took samples from each tank and will see if I can find a match on the wrench. I am fairly certain this was the instrument that was used to bash those valves off. Another interesting fin—just bagged it." Nicholas removed a bag from his jacket and held it up for Detective Tomkins to see. "What do you think, boss? Look like a burned-up Zippo lighter to you?"

Shae took the bag and carefully examined it for several minutes. When he turned the bagged lighter over, he read the single word: "Forever."

"Lieutenant Myers, I believe you are right. Looks like we are looking at arson and homicide here. Have you spoken to anyone about this yet?" Detective Tomkins handed the bag back to the investigator.

"Of course not. I knew you wouldn't want any leaks to the media, especially since all signs point to arson and homicide." Shae glanced at his watch. He had plenty of time. "Thank you, Lieutenant Myers. I am going to walk the grounds and look around a bit more. I want you to go to the lab immediately and start processing your samples—and then contact me ASAP. If you can get me the results within six hours, there is a shiny penny in it for you. No, seriously, man, get me the fucking results by four thirty—that gives you an hour to get back to the lab—and you will have an extra two hundred dollars in your droopy lab coat pocket and the recommendation you need for the FBI crime lab position you applied for. And don't tell anyone about the testing. You will have to make something up. Do we have a deal?"

"Okay, Detective. We have a deal. I didn't know you knew I was looking into that position. You are a man of divine sight, sir."

Shae chuckled. "Nicholas, you can't hide anything from the law."

The two men shook hands, and Shae walked around the farm, looking for anything that could tie Brenda to the crime. He had decided to do more than kick around the idea that Brenda was the person responsible for this, and there was no time to waste. *If that damned gut feeling of mine is right, there are others who better be looking over their shoulders.* As he walked the grid, he couldn't stop thinking about the lighter. He was sure the lighter was the key to it all. *Forever ... really? How am I going to find out who that lighter belonged to?*

After two hours, and no new discoveries, the detective

looked at his watch. *Eleven thirty—gotta get back to the station. Come on, Detective. Give me something to bring that bitch in!*

Shae arrived at the station and noticed a black Caprice Classic in his parking space. "Son of a bitch! You pricks cannot follow the rules even in a police department parking lot!" Shae turned the wheel on his car, squealed the tires, and headed for the street.

Once inside the police department, the detective stormed through the hallways—still aggravated by the schmuck in his parking space—and headed toward his office.

The pretty, big-busted secretary got up from behind her desk and nervously followed him down the hallway. "Detective Tomkins, there is someone waiting in your office … a Detective Joseph Scarth from Jackson."

As Shae reached his office, he turned around and said, "Thank you, Ms. Perkins. Sincere apologies for my rudeness." He entered his office and closed the door behind him.

The man in the chair beside Shae's desk stood. "Hello, Detective Tomkins. I am Detective Joseph Scarth from Jackson."

They shook hands.

"Good day to you, Detective. Let's get right down to it. What can we do for each other?"

Walking toward the window, straightening the creases on his navy-blue dress shirt, the young detective began to tell Shae about the condition of the Sherrill's farm.

When Detective Scarth began describing the missing family photo, Shae said, "Wait … back up, Detective. How do you know there was a photo missing? Maybe they were planning on hanging a picture there and never got the chance. Just because you saw an empty nail on the wall doesn't mean there was once something hanging there."

With a sheepish grin, he replied, "I am not done yet, Detective Tomkins. Let me finish, will ya?"

Shae got comfortable in his chair and listened to Joseph for several more minutes.

When Detective Scarth finished, he sat in the chair and sighed. "I have to be honest with you, Detective Tomkins. I am new at this. The only thing I have experience with is my gut feeling, and all signs point to this psycho Brenda."

Detective Tomkins turned in his chair and stared at the ceiling, lost in thought. "Could it really be this easy to find the killer of the three Sherrills and Adam Petersen?"

Joseph said, "Pardon me, Detective Tomkins, are you speaking to me? Are you with me here, son?"

Shae turned toward Joseph, stopped the chair, and stood. "Let's get right down to it, Detective Scarth. It is just you and me in this office. Give it to me straight. Is it safe to assume that you think Brenda Sherrill is responsible for the deaths of Donnie, Bernard, Ruby, and Adam Petersen? Because from where I was sitting, it sure sounded like your finger is pointed at her."

Joseph got up from his chair and walked toward Shae. "Yes, Detective Tomkins. I feel very strongly about Brenda Sherrill being the party responsible for all four senseless deaths. And I believe she plans to spill more blood. Brenda Sherrill is a psychopath, and I think she is more dangerous than the Iraq soldiers you fought overseas. The only thing is—how do we catch her?"

The men stood in front of the bay windows for quite some time, lost in thought.

Shae said, "I ran Brenda's license number through the system, and her record is squeaky clean. She does not have so much as a parking ticket since she started driving at sixteen years old. At first, I thought it was a mistake. I ran her license number four more times and found nothing. My sister, Kathleen Tanner, is a bigwig at Canyon Heights Memorial. I may have mentioned my suspicions about Brenda last week at my niece's birthday party. I was not all that surprised to find that Mrs. Sherrill spent a little time on the Canyon Heights Memorial psych ward last year after she miscarried. I could go on and on, Scarth, but I do not think I need to. Bottom line, Detective? I believe Brenda is a dangerous criminal, and I want to nail her to the wall in town square, but we have to proceed very carefully. Her father is Michael Miller, the mayor of New Berry Falls and a decorated Vietnam vet, for God's sake! So, my question to you, Detective Scarth, is this: How do we move forward? We have to be so careful, sir!"

Shae walked away from the window and tapped his right index finger on his nose. "I have it! I pulled Brenda over on Saturday night when I was leaving work. As the light turned green, I started to turn as she blew the red light. I didn't know it was her until I approached the car and saw her. I, of course, didn't give her a ticket. I have had plenty of that shitty paperwork before I made detective—not to mention I figured that poor family has been through so much already—and I didn't want to add to their grief. I decided to let her go, but I did tell her I wanted her to call me so we could set up a time for her to come to the police station to answer some routine questions about Tom's accident. She still hasn't called, and frankly, it pisses me off a bit. Here is what I propose, Joseph. I can go out to the Peterson farm and look around a bit more to see if there is something we missed. Really what I am doing is making an excuse to go to the Sherrill home and speak with Brenda. Their property is next to Adam Peterson's farm. It will be the perfect cover. If her car is in the driveway, I am going to stop and have a little chat with our suspect. In my experience, surprise is the best way to catch a rat—even one as beautiful and clever as Brenda Sherrill. What do you think?"

A smile formed on Scarth's face. Nodding his head, he said, "Why, Detective Tomkins, I do believe we have ourselves a plan. If you see anything pertinent to our investigation, use this to take pictures." Joseph reached into his shirt pocket, pulled out a black pen, and handed it to Shae.

Detective Tomkins said, "Really? I have been wanting one of these camera pens for months. CHPD is so damn cheap that my requests have been repeatedly ignored. Show me how it works, and I will get the goods on our pretty little nutcase."

Scarth showed his fellow officer how to operate the camera on the pen. "Easy, right, Shae? You got this. By the way, you can keep the pen, my friend. I purchased three of these nifty pens from the internet. Yep, Jackson PD is cheap as hell—just like CHPD."

The two men laughed for a few moments and decided to speak after Shae's visit with Brenda. Shae walked Joseph out, shook his hand, and watched as the young detective opened the door to the Caprice Classic in his parking space. "Son of a bitch! Young punk! Figures."

Shae shook his head, laughed, and walked back into the police department to grab a bottle of water before leaving for the farm.

As Shae drove by the Sherrill home, he noticed Brenda's car in the driveway. He decided to stop now rather than later since he didn't want to take the chance of her leaving and missing his opportunity to snoop around. He pulled into the driveway and parked behind the suspected killer's car. As he walked past the creepy vehicle, he noticed a red fingerprint on the driver's side door handle. He quickly took out the fingerprint kit from his coat pocket, placed a piece of the lifting tape on the handle, and pulled the print. He placed the tape in the envelope and put the kit in his pocket. As he started up the porch steps, the front door opened.

Brenda was smiling from ear to ear. She looked lovely in the sunlight. Her hair was long and dark, hugging the curves of her beautiful cheeks. Shae thought it was a shame that someone so pretty could be such a murderous bitch.

"Hello, Detective Tomkins. What brings you by on this glorious day? Please come in."

Shae wiped his shoes on the welcome mat before entering the home. As he walked in the door, he noticed a pair of hiking boots with a dark substance on the right boot. He turned his attention from the boot so Brenda wouldn't see that he noticed, but he wanted a better look later. "Glorious indeed, Mrs. Sherrill. How are you and little Dillon doing? I suspect you two are feeling a bit out of sorts with Tom in the hospital. I sure hope you are both getting along okay."

Shutting the door, she had an eerie smile on her face. "Me and my boy are just fine, Detective Tomkins—and please call me Brenda. May I offer you something to drink?"

Shae looked around and said, "No, thank you, Brenda. I have a bottle of water in the car. I appreciate the offer though. I am on a tight schedule today. I will get right to the point of my visit. I was on my way to the Peterson farm to wrap up a few things. I saw your car and thought I would stop by to get those routine questions answered I told you about when I saw you on Saturday evening. With all your poor family has been experiencing lately, you must have forgotten to call me. I was obliged to stop for a quick chat. I sure hope my unexpected visit isn't putting you out or keeping you from anything."

When she turned from him, to walk to the counter, he noticed her right hand was wrapped with gauze and medical tape.

Brenda took her glass from the counter, motioning for the detective to sit at the table. "Heavens no. We are always happy to do our part for the CHPD."

As Shae took his notebook out of his pocket, the fingerprint kit fell to the floor.

Brenda reached down, picked it up, and handed it to him. Her pretty smile instantly turned into a frown.

Shae wanted to smack himself for being so stupid and dropping his kit.

Dillon started crying in the nursery upstairs, but Brenda acted like she didn't hear him. She sat in her chair with a blank look on her face.

Shae touched her hand and gave it a light shake. "Brenda, dear, are you okay?"

No answer—just that weird stare.

"Brenda, are you okay? Do you hear Dillon crying?"

She snapped out of it, looked at him, and forced a smile. "Oh my goodness. Yes, I hear him, Detective Tomkins. I am extra tired with Tom being away and the stress. Please excuse me while I go see what his fussing is all about."

As she disappeared up the stairs, Shae took the pen out of his pocket, turned it on, and quickly began to look around the room. As he walked by the living room, he noticed three oak cabinets with glass doors mounted to the far-left wall. He walked closer to the wall and was pleased to see that all three cabinets contained Zippo lighters. *Someone in the house has one hell of a collection.* He snapped several pictures with Scarth's pen, taking note and a close-up of the third cabinet, which had an empty spot right in the very middle of the cabinet. *Bingo!* He snapped a few pictures of the empty space. Hearing sounds coming from the nursery, he walked to the stairs. "Brenda, I just received a call from headquarters. I have to run. I have everything I need. I will call you if I have any questions. I will show myself out. Please enjoy your day. I will be praying for Tom's speedy recovery."

She appeared at the top of the stairs with Dillon in her arms. "Thank you, Detective. Be safe out there—and have a fabulous day."

He walked toward the door and paused to look at the hiking boots. *Fuck it.* He picked up both boots and hurried out to his car. He opened the door, put the boots on the passenger floor, and sped off. Looking back at the house, he could see Brenda watching him through a second-floor window.

Once he was clear from Brenda's evil, creepy stare, Shae picked up his cell phone. He was pleased to see it was four fifteen. Shae knew Nicholas Myers would still be at the lab. He also knew he had better stop at the bank and withdraw two hundred clams because Nick never missed out on the opportunity to make an extra buck. He dialed the number.

"Nicholas Myers here."

Shae never understood why people answered the phone as if they did not know who was calling them. Nick had Shae's number for as long as the number was his.

"Hey, Nick. Shae here. Any word on the wrench you found at the Peterson farm?"

Swallowing the last bite of the turkey and Swiss hoagie his wife had packed in his lunchbox that morning, the investigator said, "You have impeccable timing, Detective. I just got the results back—and we have a winner! The wrench has metal residue matching the metal from all three propane tanks. I attempted to pull a sample off of all three propane tanks to see if there if there was any possibility there may be a match to the wrench on the tanks, but of course, the fire destroyed any evidence of metal from the wrench. However, it is very safe to assume the wrench was the culprit that broke the valves on the tanks at the Peterson farm. Unfortunately, there was only one print pulled from the lighter. I was able to get my hands on Tom Sherrill's print, and it isn't his."

Detective Tomkins was silent for a few moments as he thought about the mystery fingerprint. "Okay, Nick, I am on my way to the lab now. See you soon."

Nick was waiting for Shae when he arrived. He held the door open for him as he entered the lab.

Detective Tomkins pulled $200 from his back pocket and handed it to Nicholas. "You did a great job, kid. I always appreciate your help. I will start working on your recommendation."

The young investigator shook his head. "Why do I sense there is something else you need, Shae?"

Laughing, the detective replied, "See, that is why you are the best investigator in Canyon Heights, my friend. You are very intuitive and wise. Yes, there is another issue. I am afraid I did something that could potentially get me into a lot of trouble."

Scratching the back of his head, Nick looked at Shae and said, "Okay, enough ass-kissing. Tell me what you did and how I can help."

Detective Tomkins began his story, starting with why he stopped at Brenda's and how he saw the hiking boots with the dark substance on the right boot. He then went on to confess that he could not resist taking them on his way out the door.

"Holy shit, Shae! Are you fucking crazy? You know you can't just take someone's belongings without a warrant! What the hell do you want me to do? Sprinkle fairy dust on them or wave my magic wand so the will appear where you stole them from?"

Detective Tomkins started to pace, rubbing his fingers through his dark hair, and sweat beads appeared on his forehead. "I know. I really screwed up! She is our killer, Nick, and I need to have the dark substance on that right boot tested. If I am correct, it is blood—and it will match the blood type of Bernard Sherrill. What I am asking you to do will not get you into hot water. If I am found out, I will say you knew nothing about the illegal seizure of the boots. However, here is the catch: you have to take the sample right now so I can get the boots back to where they came from before our pretty little murderer realizes they are missing. I need you to do this for me, Nick. I need you to do this for the family and the poor folks who have lost their lives to that psychotic bitch! We have to stop her before she takes another innocent life!"

The investigator walked over to his desk, pulled out the chair, sat down, and rested his head in his hands. "Okay, Shae. Give me the boot. I will run the test right now. You owe me big-time!"

The detective took a large latex glove from the box on Nicholas's desk and walked out of the door. Moments later, he appeared with Brenda's right boot. Holding it up with a gloved hand, he asked, "Where do you want me to put this?"

Motioning for the detective to follow him, Nicholas replied, "Come with me, you pain in the ass."

The two men walked through the double, stainless steel doors to the lab.

Pointing to a long table next to an evidence-drying cabinet, Nick said, "Put the boot on this table gently. Do you know the blood type of Mr. Sherrill?" Shae placed the boot on the table, removed the glove, and threw it in the garbage can next to the door. He reached in his pocket and pulled out his notebook. After flipping through a few pages, he said, "Bernard's blood type was AB negative. Isn't that pretty rare?"

The investigator was taking pictures of the substance on the boot. "Yes, it is. In fact, it is the rarest blood type of all. Let me briefly explain to you how I am going to determine the blood type on this boot. First, I need to be sure the substance is blood. To do that, I have taken pictures of the substance with this hyperspectral imaging camera. According to these images, the mystery substance is, indeed, blood." Taking a Q-tip from the drawer of the cabinet beside the table, the investigator began to swab the substance gently. He placed it in a glass tube, sealed it with a small lid, and placed it on a metal tray next to the camera. Once the task was complete, he returned to his desk and sat down, taking a drink from a bottle of water. "I will do some chemical testing on the Q-tip to determine what blood type it is. I will know what the blood type is in twenty-four hours. Is there anything else I can do for you, sir?"

Reaching back into his coat pocket, he pulled out the fingerprint kit and the envelope with the bloody print inside. "I lifted this print from the handle on the driver's side door of our suspect's car. Please find out if there is a print in our database that matches the blood type. I am going to tell you right now that you won't find any prints in the database that match, but at least you can get the blood type for me."

Myers rose from his chair, walked to the long table, and placed the envelope by the tube with the Q-tip. "Okay, Shae. I will start on the chemical testing before I leave for the day and complete the rest in the morning when I get to the lab. As soon as I have the information, I will contact you. Now, if I were you, I would get these boots back to their rightful owner."

Detective Tomkins patted Nick on the back. "Thank you, buddy. I really appreciate your help with this. Please remember not to breathe a word of this to anyone."

The two men walked to the doors together and shook hands.

Once Shae was in his car, he thought about how he was going to get the boots back inside Brenda's house. Looking around, he saw a market across the street. Shae started the car and headed to the market to do some shopping.

Arriving at Tom and Brenda's house, Shae could see she was home. Before he pulled down the driveway, he placed the boots in the half-filled grocery bag. "Perfect cover," he said as he started toward the house. He parked behind Brenda's car again. This time, when he walked past the vehicle, the red fingerprint was gone.

He walked up the front porch steps and knocked on the door.

He could hear Dillon crying as Brenda opened up the door. "Hi again, Detective Tomkins. Two times in one day? I feel so popular. Please shut the door and come in. Pardon me while I collect my son." As she hurried off to collect the baby, Shae took the boots out of the grocery bag and put them in the exact place where he had taken them that morning. He walked to the kitchen as Brenda entered with Dillon in her arms.

She said, "What can I do for you, Detective?"

Shae placed the grocery bag on the counter. "Well, with Tom being in the hospital, I thought you might not have time to shop. I picked up a few snacks, bread, milk, and a bottle of red wine. I noticed the empty bottle on the counter earlier today and figured you may be out. As a new mama, a glass of wine at the end of a long day is a must."

She laughed, tossed her hair to the side, and said, "How nice of you. Who would have ever thought Canyon Heights's finest would be making a special delivery to little old me." The smile on her beautiful face disappeared as she got up from her chair. "Now, please, if that is all, I must unfortunately say goodbye. Dillon has a doctor's appointment, and we are running late. Let me walk you out."

Shae could hardly believe the change in her and immediately thought of the fingerprint that was no longer on the car.

She opened the door, and he walked through it. As he turned to say goodbye, the door slammed in his face. He was speechless as he walked down the stairs. He hurried to his car, turned the key, threw to car in reverse, and sped off.

Brenda watched until he was out of sight. She looked down to see that the hiking boots that had disappeared earlier had mysteriously reappeared.

# BREAKING THE NEWS

Joanne looked at the clock on her bedside table. "Oh my goodness! I slept until noon!" After almost falling out of bed, she ran to the bathroom, took off her nightgown, and got into the shower. She was irritated with herself for sleeping so late. She had planned on getting to the hospital early to see Tom. She was worried that one of his brothers or maybe his sister would end up telling him about the death of his parents. She knew what losing them would do to him. Even though she made sure to tell the staff on Tom's floor to keep quiet about Bernard and Ruby's deaths, she knew it could still happen. Joanne didn't want to tell him, but she knew she had to be the one to break the news. How would she do it? Joanne had no clue how to tell Tom the parents he loved and adored were both dead. Today would be one of the worst days of her life.

When Joanne got off the elevator, she heard the heart-wrenching screams of a man. She reached room 205, took a deep breath, and walked inside. She was shocked that Tom was not in his bed.

As she exited the room, two nurses ran by her. One of the nurses had a long syringe. Joanne turned around and followed them. She heard one of the nurses say, "Mr. Sherrill please come with us and we will explain everything to you."

**TAMI BOYER**

When Joanne ran to the room, Tom was sobbing on the floor. "No! No!"

Joanne looked up and saw the television. It was an exclusive report from the Sherrill farm. She ran over to Tom, pushed the nurse's hand away, and said, "I am Tom's sister. Help me get him to his feet." She turned to the other nurse. "Miss, please get me a wheelchair so we can get him back to his room."

Tom looked up at her through his tears.

She rubbed his back, kissed his face, and said, "Tom, I am here. Please calm down. If you don't get a hold of yourself, you are going to end up in the psych ward. Let's get you back to your room and settled. I will tell you everything, but you have to calm down, honey."

The nurse finally arrived with the wheelchair, and the three of them got Tom into the chair. "Thank you, ladies. Now please let me take care of my brother. I will ring the nurse's station if we need anything." Joanne grabbed the wheelchair's handles and started for Tom's room. His deep sobs were so painful that she began to cry.

All at once, Tom started to vomit.

Joanne took off her sweater and wiped his mouth and chest with it.

When they reached his room, Tom got up from the chair and turned on the television.

Joanne walked to the corner and pulled out the plug.

As the television went black, he fell to his knees.

She sat on the floor and held his head in her arms.

Thirty minutes later, Tom's sobbing subsided. Looking up at Joanne, he said, "Where is Brenda? Why isn't she here? Is she okay?"

Remembering that the doctor told her Tom might have some short-term memory loss, she didn't know what to say.

She stood up and walked toward the door, tears falling steadily from her eyes. She began to speak just as Dr. Nagy and the nurse walked into the room.

The nurse helped Tom off the floor, led him back to his bed, and placed the IV in his arm. "It's okay, Tom. We are taking good care of you. You have had a serious head injury. Please try to relax and sleep for a bit." She removed a syringe from her pocket and injected the IV with its contents before exiting the room.

Dr. Nagy turned to Joanne and said, "Mrs. Roberts, please come with me."

Tom was drifting off to sleep. Taking his hand in hers, she leaned down and softly kissed his forehead. "I will be back, Tommy. You get some sleep. Rest, sweetie. We will talk more later. I love you." She followed Dr. Nagy out of the room, wiping warm tears from her cheeks.

In the hallway, the doctor looked at Joanne and said, "We have to figure out a way to tell Tom about the past few weeks. He is experiencing some short-term memory loss as expected. He keeps asking for his wife, and we do not know what to tell him. Why has she not been here with her husband? I feel there is something that I am not being told, and if there is, you need to come clean with it now. I can tell by looking at you that something is amiss. Please, if I am going to help Tom get back to himself, I need to know the truth, Mrs. Roberts. Unlike some people in the medical field, I actually got into this field to help others. I didn't go to college all those years to make money, and my reputation is impeccable. You can trust me. I will not say a word to anyone, but you must tell me what is going on. I need to know what to say to him when he is begging us for his wife."

Through the tears, she replied, "Is there a place where

we can talk privately? This is going to take a while—plus I am feeling like I am going to pass out."

The doctor took her hand and led her to his office. He opened a small refrigerator, took out two bottles of water, and handed one to Joanne. "Okay, I am ready. Please tell me what is going on."

Joanne placed the water bottle on the table and rubbed her legs nervously. Finally, with a deep breath, she said, "First of all, please call me Joanne. I feel so incredibly old when people call me Mrs. Roberts. I am on the edge with all that has happened the last couple of weeks, Dr. Nagy. My brother is dead. Tom is hurt, and his son and parents are dead. I feel like I am having a nightmare I can't wake up from. It is important for you to know that I am not Tom's sister. Detective Shae Tomkins told the nurse on duty that I was Tom's sister so I could get information about his condition at any time. I am the one who found him at the bottom of my brother's root cellar." Joanne told the tale that had consumed her life for the last few weeks. By the time she was finished, an hour and fifteen minutes had passed.

Dr. Nagy shook his head, cleared his throat, and said, "I am off duty, Joanne. I don't know about you, but I sure could use a drink. Are you game?" He walked over to the cabinet, took out two glasses and a bottle of whiskey, and sat down next to her.

Joanne looked at him, cocked her head, and said, "I am way past ready, Doctor. I am sorry to drag you into this mess. I am new at this kind of thing, and I am tired, sad and genuinely pissed off at the whole mess."

The doctor filled each glass halfway and handed one to Joanne. He drank his quickly, picked up the bottle, and filled his glass. "Okay, so what do we do now, Joanne? Do you think Tom's crazy wife will show up here and try to kill him? Should I alert security or call the police?"

She got up from the chair, drinking the last of the whiskey, and put the glass on the table. "As of now, Brenda is the only suspect. She hasn't been arrested or even questioned at the police station as far as I am aware. The police are being very cautious because her father is the mayor of New Berry Falls. It isn't going to be easy putting the daughter of such a good and influential man in prison. I am going to go to the Sherrill house after I check on Tom. I want to see if she is still in town. Who knows—maybe the crazy bitch killed her son and herself too. I can't say I would be upset if I walked in that house and found her hanging from the chandelier. If she did kill herself, I sure hope she took the baby next door first. Dr. Nagy, if she comes here and tries to see Tom, she can't be alone in the room with him. She already tried to kill him once, and I am betting she plans to try it again. Can you have him moved to another room? Is it possible to put a security guard close by so he is safe?"

The doctor drank the rest of his whiskey, got up from his chair, and after a little wobble, placed the empty glasses in the sink. "The only way to keep him safe is to have Tom moved to the psych ward. I will make sure Brenda's name isn't on the list so she can't gain entry to the locked ward. In fact, I think, in his case, there should only be a few names on Tom's visitor list. Besides your name, who else should be allowed to have access to Tom?"

After a few moments, Joanne said, "I think it would be a good idea to put Detective Tomkins and Detective Joseph Scarth on the list. I think the three of us are the only people who should be allowed access to Tom. I fear others in the family will cause unneeded stress, and right now, according to you, that would be a bad thing for him."

Dr. Nagy called the nurses' station to begin Tom's transfer. "Okay, Joanne. He will be moved to the psych ward within the hour. If you want to see him before you leave, you should go now. You have my cell number if there is anything you find out that you think I should know."

Joanne shook Dr. Nagy's hand, and then she hugged him.

He looked at her with surprise and kissed her cheek. "Please be safe when you go to Brenda's house—and call my cell phone after you leave. I need to be sure you are safe. My patient's recovery depends on it. Now, please go see Tom and assure him that everything will be okay. Thank you for your honesty, Joanne. I will see you soon."

She walked to Tom's room, and she could hear that he was talking to a female. She peeked around the door, and Brenda was sitting next to him on the bed. The panic was overwhelming, and Joanne ran back to the elevator. She ran to the doctor's office and began beating on it. "Dr. Nagy? Dr. Nagy! It's Joanne. Open up—quick!"

He opened the door and said, "What in the world is the trouble, Joanne? What happened? Is Tom okay?"

Joanne was pacing and rubbing her hands together nervously. "Brenda is in Tom's room! You have to get her out of there now!"

Dr. Nagy picked up the phone and instructed the nurse to go to Tom's room at once and ask Brenda to leave. He told the nurse to tell her that Tom is resting to prepare for testing later. "Joanne, go down the back stairs—now. I am going to go down and speak with her. I will keep her busy for a while so you can go check her house and see if there is anything you can use against her."

Joanne hugged Dr. Nagy and said, "Doctor-turned-detective, I appreciate your commitment to your patients and our community, Dr. Nagy. Thank you."

He looked at her with a smile and replied, "I don't like people fucking with my patients. Now get out of here so I can keep that nut from leaving." He patted her on the shoulder, assuring her everything would be okay.

Joanne turned and hurried out the door, dropping her purse. She picked it up and ran toward the stairwell without noticing that her wallet had fallen out of her purse.

When Dr. Nagy got down to the second floor, Brenda was arguing with the supervising nurse. He held out his hand to Brenda as he approached. "Hi there. I am Dr. Nagy, one of your husband's doctors. It is good to finally meet you. There is so much we need to talk about in regard to Tom's condition from the time he was admitted to his present situation. Such a severe injury in any case is dangerous, but one to the head like in Tom's case can traumatize the patient, physically and emotionally, for years—and, in some cases, for life."

Brenda said, "It is good to meet you, Doctor. I don't understand why I can't stay with my husband during the testing. Is there someone I can speak to about it?"

The doctor sighed. "I am the physician in charge, Brenda, so you can speak to me. Why don't we go to my office and have a chat?"

Brenda took a hold of his arm and said, "Lead the way, Dr. Nagy."

With a smile on his face and a chill running through his body, he said, "Okay then. Off we go."

Arriving at his office, the doctor opened the door for Brenda. Pointing at the chair across from his desk, he said, "Please, Brenda, have a seat. I have to excuse myself for a few minutes. Make yourself comfortable. There is water in the fridge, and the coffee on the counter is fresh. The cups are in the cupboard above the coffeemaker."

"Thank you, Dr. Nagy. I could use a cup of coffee. Take your time. I will be here."

He walked out of the office and shut the door behind him.

After she poured her coffee, she walked around the office and looked at the certificates and medical licenses on the walls. The doctor had a collection of antique knives in the cabinet by the restroom. She counted eighty-one in all. As she made her way back to the chair, she noticed something on the floor next to the door. She walked over and picked it up. The lambskin wallet was soft and appeared to be new. She opened it, and what she saw made her blood boil. The object of her anger was a license. "Joanne Roberts! That bitch!" She put the wallet into her jacket pocket, placed the coffee cup on the counter, and started for the door.

Dr. Nagy opened the door, startling Brenda. He said, "Oh my goodness! I am sorry I scared you. There will be no more interruptions, my dear. Please sit so we can talk about Tom."

As he walked past her, she could smell the whiskey on his breath. "I apologize, Dr. Nagy. I am a bit jumpy lately with everything that has happened in the past few weeks. Our family appreciates everything that you and the good staff here at Canyon Heights Memorial are doing for Tom. It is wonderful to know that my husband is in good hands. Has anyone else had the pleasure of chatting with you and drinking your marvelous coffee?"

With a puzzled look, he replied, "No, ma'am. I don't have many people in my office, and I rarely share my secret brew." He got up from his chair and said, "I lied, Brenda.

I have one more interruption. I am afraid my secret brew has gotten the best of me. Please excuse me while I use the restroom." He walked to the restroom and closed the door.

She was furious with Dr. Nagy for lying to her. She knew Joanne had been in his office and wondered why he had lied about it. Without thinking, she went to the cabinet and selected the largest knife. When the toilet flushed, Brenda hurried back to her chair. She had a firm hold of the knife inside the sleeve of her jacket.

Dr. Nagy opened the door and said, "Okay, no more coffee for me." He laughed and made himself comfortable behind his desk.

Brenda placed Joanne's wallet on the desk in front of the doctor. "If nobody has been in your office, Dr. Nagy, how do you explain this wallet I found by your door?"

The look on his face was a mixture of panic and fear as he picked up the wallet and opened it.

Before he could answer, Brenda slid across the desk and sunk the knife into his neck, twisting it as he fought her. The blood squirted from his neck all over her and onto the desk. It didn't take him long to bleed out. Once he had taken his last breath, she got up from the desk and looked at him for several minutes. "That's what you get for being a fucking liar." She went into the restroom to clean the blood off her face.

Joanne decided to park at Peterson's farm and walk to the Sherrill's house. She didn't want to take the chance of Brenda coming home and seeing her car in the driveway.

She walked up the steps to the front porch and tried the doorknob to see if Brenda had left the door open.

She wasn't surprised to find the door locked. She looked under the mat and the plants near the door before spotting a large cactus with a small "Home Sweet Home" sign in the soil. Tears fell from her eyes because she knew who the sign really belonged to. She was the one who had given the sign to her brother, and she knew Brenda had killed him. She picked up the cactus and saw the key. "Twisted psycho," she said as she bent down and took the key, gently placing the pot back on the ground.

Once inside the house, her eyes were immediately drawn to the dining room table. As she got closer to the table, her eyes grew wider—and the hairs on the back of her neck stood up. In the middle of the table, there was a family picture. It was the last Sherrill family picture that would ever be taken. She picked it up and gasped when she noticed that the picture had an addition. Dillon's first baby photo had been cut and pasted into Brenda's arms.

Joanne gently placed the picture back on the table, took out her phone, and took several pictures of the frame, its contents, and the surroundings. Once she had what she wanted, she wiped her prints from the bottom two corners of the frame and headed toward the front door.

As she reached for the doorknob, she heard the sound of a car door slamming. She ran to the window and was horrified to see Brenda walking up the front walk. Joanne darted for the back door, looking over her shoulder as she fled. At the end of the Sherrill property, she bolted through the cornfield and ran for her life.

# CRUMBLING WALLS

Joanne bounded through the end of the cornfield and sprinted for her car. As she rounded the side porch, she heard a sound that made her stop and hold her breath.

She crouched beside the house, near the outside entrance to the root cellar. The car came to a stop right beside Joanne's car. The driver got out, leaving the car running and the headlights on. When the car's owner hurried past the headlights, she could see it was Brenda. "Fuck," Joanne said quietly.

Brenda ran through the police tape, kicking debris out of her way as she charged through the mess to the front porch stairs. As she hurried up the steps, she yelled, "Joanne? Joanne! Where are you? I know you were in my house, bitch! And I know you are here somewhere. You sure as hell didn't leave without your car. Did you like our family picture? Too bad you won't be able to tell anyone about it. Dead sluts can't talk."

Joanne looked around for something to defend herself with, but there was nothing in the immediate area that she could use. She stood up and leaned against the house, thinking of how she was going to get out of this without dying. All of a sudden, the look on Joanne's face turned from panic and fear to a sweet, calm, happy smile. Giggling to herself, she said, "Okay, Adam. Big brother, let's see if they found your end-of-the-world stash." She crawled to the entrance of the root cellar. Taking the hairpin from her hair, she began to pry the bottom board away from the structure. Once the board was freed, she pulled out a metal box from inside the narrow wall of the entrance.

She paused, listening to the crazy rampage that was still happening inside of what was once the Peterson family home. She looked down at the box, shaking her head and smiling as she opened it. "Thanks, big brother. You're still looking out for me." She put her hand in the box and pulled out the M1911 pistol her brother had used to defend himself in Korea when his plane went down. He never talked about what happened that day. The only thing she ever heard him say was that his sidearm had saved his life.

"Well, today, Adam, it just might save mine." The magazine was fully loaded, and there was a bullet in the chamber. She took two more loaded magazines from the box and placed them in her pocket. As she flicked off the safety, she heard the screaming cries of a baby.

"Oh my God. She brought Dillon with her." She watched as Brenda ran to the car.

Brenda opened the back door, took Dillon out of his car seat, cradled him in her arms, and rocked him. "It's okay, sweet angel. Mommy is here, dear boy. I am going to take you to Grandma and Grandpa's house so I can button things up around here—and then we will leave this place forever." She kissed the baby's forehead, placed him securely in his car seat, and closed the door. She turned toward the Peterson and called out into the darkness, "Joanne, you slimy skank, you won't get away from me. I will be back for you, so slither away and hide, little slut, because I am coming for you." Brenda got behind the wheel, closed the door, and sped off.

Joanne was quiet for several minutes to be sure Brenda was gone. She slowly walked toward the front of the house with the pistol in her hand. She stood under the tree by her car and waited a few moments before opening the door. After she was inside the car and the doors were locked, she flicked the safety on and put the gun on the passenger seat.

Knowing she was Brenda's next victim, Joanne decided she couldn't go home. She pulled down the visor and called Detective Joseph. The dispatcher on the other end told Joanne that Detective Scarth had been called away to Canyon Heights on an emergency. She knew not to ask for any information, thanked the dispatcher, and pressed end on her phone. She quickly dialed CHPD and asked for Detective Shae Tomkins. When dispatch didn't answer and she was directly sent to an automated voice mail system, Joanne was filled with a terrible feeling in her stomach. She stepped hard on the gas pedal and headed for Canyon Heights Memorial.

When Joanne arrived at the hospital, the parking lot was full of police cars. Their lights illuminated the evening sky. Cops and officials were everywhere. She stopped the car momentarily to see if she could spot anywhere to park, and there was a startling knock on her window.

Detective Shae Tomkins motioned for her to roll down the window. "Joanne, please pull your car over to the right where the officer is moving the barrier for your entry. I will meet you there."

She turned off the car and waited for the detective. When she saw Shae approaching, she got out of the car.

He shook her hand and said, "Thank you for stopping to talk with me. May I ask what you are doing here at this time of evening? I think I have an idea, but why don't you tell me."

Joanne liked Detective Tomkins, but she was in no mood for cop antics. Joanne began her story from her chat with Dr. Nagy, Brenda showing up to the hospital, sneaking into the Sherrill home, and the freak show she just witnessed at the Peterson farm. "Detective Tomkins, after I couldn't reach you or Detective Scarth, I had a horrible feeling something had happened here. It turns out I am right. Now it's your turn, sir. What in the hell is going on?"

Shae turned to look at the sea of red lights that flooded the hospital parking lot. Shaking his head, he said, "Yes, I am right about why you are here, Joanne, and I am very sorry to tell you that Dr. Nagy is dead. All signs point to Brenda Sherrill as his killer. Detective Scarth is interviewing witnesses in the hospital. Our departments are working together on this since we have a common suspect. I believe you are already aware." She let out a gasp and collapsed in his arms.

Several police officers ran over to carry Joanne into the hospital on a gurney.

She woke up inside the emergency room.

Shae said, "Joanne, are you okay?"

She sat up and sighed as she watched the other officer walk off to find a doctor. "Yes, I am alive. I can't say I am okay. I am obviously not okay. What happened? Brenda killed Dr. Nagy? Did I hear you correctly?"

Shae put his hand on Joanne's shoulder, rubbing her gently and trying to console her. "Be still for a bit, drink some water, see what the doctor says, and then we will talk. I have to excuse myself a few minutes. I see the doctor walking this way now. After he checks you out, I will come back so we can talk. Seriously, you're no good to me like this. So just stay put." Before she could say anything, Shae was gone.

The doctor had Joanne moved into a private room. One

nurse asked the routine emergency room questions, and the other took her vitals and drew some blood.

Thirty minutes after the nurses left the room, there was a knock on the door.

"Joanne, may we come in?" Detective Tomkins asked.

She sat up on the table and said, "Yes."

Detective Tomkins walked in with Dr. Steven Hammond.

Shae took a seat in the corner, and Dr. Hammond said, "First, Mrs. Roberts, I need to ask you if it is okay that Detective Tomkins is sitting in with us. Do we have your permission?"

She looked at Shae and then back at the doctor. "Of course—whatever I can do to help. Doctor, I feel fine and would like to leave. Let's get to it so I can get the hell out of here—please."

Dr. Hammond looked at her sternly. "Your tests are fine, but your blood pressure is a little high. From what I understand, it is probably related to stress. I have prescribed ten milligrams of Valium. Take them every four hours as needed. Please follow up with your primary physician and call me with any questions or problems you may have in the meantime." Dr. Hammond handed her his business card and headed toward the door.

Detective Tomkins got up and walked after him. "Please wait, Dr. Hammond. If it is okay with Joanne, I would like it if you would sit here with us while I ask her a few questions. If she becomes upset and passes out, I need someone here with me. Is that okay with you, Joanne? Dr. Hammond?"

Joanne and the doctor looked at each other—and then at Shae—and nodded.

Detective Tomkins took a tape recorder out of his coat pocket and placed it on the counter next to the bed where

Joanne was sitting. He hit play and began. "This is Detective Shae Tomkins. I am here at Canyon Heights Memorial with Joanne Roberts and Dr. Steven Hammond. I am speaking with Joanne in regard to the events that took place today, Thursday March 31, 2016. Joanne, please describe what happened from the time you got off the elevator to see Tom until this moment."

Joanne told every sad, terrible detail of her day.

At the end of her story, Detective Tomkins asked, "Can you please confirm for me the complete name of the person whom Dr. Nagy left his office to meet at the nurses' station on the second floor of Canyon Heights Memorial?"

Joanne said, "Yes I can, her name is Brenda Sherrill, and she is a coldhearted, murdering bitch!"

Shae looked at Joanne, turned off the recorder, and shook his head. "Yes, Joanne, I believe you nailed it on that one. Thank you for your time. I am so sorry for your many losses and the sad times you have endured. You may very well be saddened many more times before this is over and in the future, but know this … we will get justice for you, the Sherrill family, and the Nagy family. You will have it—that I promise you."

Dr. Hammond walked over to Joanne and said, "Did you say Brenda Sherrill?"

"Yes, I did. Why do you ask?"

The doctor looked at Shae and said, "Detective, you may want to turn your recorder back on for this."

Shae reached for his recorder and pressed play again.

# ON THE RUN

Dr. Hammond told his account of Saturday March 26, 2016. He was disappointed when Judy took the evening babysitting job. "I don't get many weekends off. Last weekend I was off and hoped to spend it with the family. When Judy came home with $150 for seven hours of babysitting a sleeping infant, I decided it was worth it for her. I have to say the whole thing was strange though. When Brenda came back to the house at midnight, her shirt was torn. Judy thought she saw blood on her shirt. Brenda assured her it was an old shirt she used for painting."

A cell phone began ringing, and the doctor and detective looked at their phones.

"Thank you, Dr. Hammond, for taking time to speak with me." He shut off the recorder. "Dr. Hammond, you have been very helpful. Please call me if you think of anything else. You have my card. I have to excuse myself and return this phone call. I will come back to speak with you when I am finished, Joanne. Is that okay?"

She looked at Dr. Hammond, "Can I leave, sir?"

Pulling several papers from a file, he said, "Yes, Mrs. Roberts. You can freshen up and get dressed. I will have your nurse get the discharge papers ready for you. Please take your time and have a good evening."

The doctor rushed off, and Detective Tomkins dialed Meyer's cell number.

"Hey, meathead. I have the results you have been waiting for. Do you want to come down to the lab or would you prefer that I put you out of your misery and read them to you over the phone?"

With a forced laugh, Shae said, "Hello to you too, Skippy. I am a busy man. I don't have time for your shit. You can read them to me right now. But could you please stop eating while you do it? God, Nick, every time I see or talk to you on the phone, you are eating. I can't believe you are so fit. I hate guys like you! Now tell me what I need to know before I throw up."

Both men laughed.

"Okay, old-timer. Pipe down. Here goes. The blood on the right hiking boot matches Bernard Sherrill 100 percent. The bloody index fingerprint didn't show up in the database, but it looked a lot like the print on the lighter. I had our fingerprint expert take a peek, and guess what? Yep, you guessed it! The print on the lighter and the print on the door handle are from the same index finger and from the same right-handed person. I decided to do a little bit more of my own investigating, and I was able to find out Brenda Sherrill's blood type is B positive, which matches the blood type from the bloody print on the door handle. I am already aware that the blood found on the driveway leading to the Sherrill's home is B positive too. What do you think of that, sir?"

Shae was smiling from ear to ear. "Great detective work,

punk! I will meet up with you this weekend. Supper and beers on me. I will have your recommendation and a few clams for you. You're going to do a fine job for the FBI. I have to go catch me a killer. So, until tomorrow, my friend." The two men hugged, patted each other on the back, and Shae hurried out the door.

Before he could dial his phone, it rang. "Detective Scarth, I was just dialing your number. I am at Canyon Heights Memorial with Joanne Roberts. I am heading to Canyon Heights PD shortly. I have all the information we need for a warrant to pick up Brenda Sherrill. Where are you?"

After the connection's static cleared, he answered, "I am on my way back to Jackson. Call me at my office when you can fill me in."

Shae was tired and thought again for a moment.

"When I get the warrant, I will send you an email with every bit of information I have—along with the warrant. Together, we got this bitch."

Detective Tomkins knocked on the door.

"Come in," Joanne said. "Hey, you. There are two police cars assigned and sitting outside your house at this very moment. They know your car, plates, everything, so they will recognize you when you pull up. They will be there until Brenda is brought in or until she is dead. I saw the nurse bring in your discharge papers. Let's get you out of here so you can get home and rest." Shae took her by the hand and led her from the hospital.

Once they arrived at her car, Shae asked, "Are you sure you are okay to drive, Joanne? I can take you home or follow you. If you would rather not be at your house, there are a few hotels nearby. I want you to be safe, and police protection is the best-case scenario in this situation. Joanne, you look exhausted. Please let's get you home."

She ran her hand through her hair. "I heard what you said on the phone to Detective Scarth about Brenda. I can get myself home, Detective Tomkins. Go catch that psycho and put her away for good where she can never hurt anyone again. Please, no matter what time it is, once you have her in custody, please call me. I want to be sure Tom is safe."

When Joanne's car was out of sight, Shae took off for his own car, already dialing his phone. "Good evening, Judge Simpson. First of all, my apologies for disturbing you at home at this late hour. I knew you would want to know the hospital where your sister works is safe, sir. We have police security covering the perimeter. We have a suspect, not in custody, but there is a strong case against her. I am heading to the CHPD right now and will email everything to you as soon as I arrive. My request is that, upon review of the evidence, you issue an arrest warrant for murder." There was no answer on the other end. "Sir, can you hear me?" Shae was about to freak out.

"Calm down, sonny. I am here. You have the warrant, but please don't email the information. I still can't figure out damn computers. I will stick with my fax machine. I will be waiting by the fax to sign the papers and fax them right back. You go make this town and others safer to live in, son. You and all those like you are an asset to the lives of all of us. Now go so I can get my old body back to bed."

With a laugh, Shae said, "Thank you, sir. It is always a pleasure."

Arriving back at the station, Shae filled out the papers for the warrant request. He printed out and faxed every piece of information he had from Canyon Heights PD and Jackson

PD along with the request. Within minutes, the warrant for the arrest of Brenda Sherrill arrived.

Brenda was almost to her parents' house when she remembered she hadn't called them to see if they could watch Dillon. She dialed the number, and her mother answered. "Hi, Mom. Do you mind watching Dillon overnight? The hospital called, and I need to be there, with Tom, for some tests." She could hear *Three's Company* on the TV in the background.

"Of course, dear. Is Tom okay? When will you be here?"

"Right now, Mom. I am outside."

Fiona walked out to help bring in her grandson. "Are you all right, honey? You look tired—a little dirty, even. What in the world is going on?"

Brenda rushed in the front door with Dillon and his gear. "Nothing's going on, Mama. I have been busy going back and forth to the hospital and taking care of the baby. Tom is fine. I have to sign papers for some tests—that's all. I will be back early tomorrow morning to pick up my boy."

Fiona was taking off Dillon's jacket and smiling. "Okay, dear. We will enjoy every second with our grandson."

Brenda took Dillon into her arms, gazed into his bright blue eyes, and kissed him gently on the forehead. "Mommy will be back for you tomorrow, sweet one." She put Dillon in her mother's arms, kissed her on the cheek, and hurried out the door.

The phone started to ring as Fiona watched her daughter drive away. With the baby still in her arms, she answered, "Hello? Miller residence."

"Good evening, Mrs. Miller. My name is Detective Joseph Scarth. I have a few questions for your daughter and haven't been able to get in contact with her. Is she staying with you while Tom is in the hospital?"

Fiona kissed Dillon's head and rubbed his cheek. "Why, yes. She was just here. Brenda said was needed at Canyon Heights Memorial. She dropped the baby off for the night."

"Thank you, Mrs. Miller. If you hear from her, could you please ask her to come see me at the police station? Then, if you wouldn't mind giving me a call, I would appreciate it so much. My cell number is 831-323-8811. Thank you so much for taking the time to speak with me."

"Let me know if there is anything else I can do for you, Detective. Have a good evening."

For a few moments, Detective Scarth rocked back and forth and tapped his pen on the desk. Grabbing his keys and cell phone, he ran out to his car. He opened the trunk and pulled out a Benelli M4 shotgun—his favorite possession and a popular weapon for Marines. "Hi ya, Betty. We aren't taking any chances with this crazy bitch." He kissed the barrel, got in his car, and placed Betty on the floor behind the passenger seat.

Just as he pulled away, his cell phone rang. "Good evening, Detective Tomkins. Gimme something good, sir!"

Shae said, "Oorah! We got the warrant on Brenda

Sherrill. Put it out there, Detective, for all to hear! Let's pick her up!"

Just as Detective Scarth was about to respond "Oorah," a car came speeding up behind him and passed him on a double yellow line. He looked at his speedometer. "Holy shit. I am doing forty-five in a twenty-five, and this asshole is passing me at fifty on a yellow double line."

Detective Tomkins yelled, "Detective Scarth! What the hell, man?"

"Oorah, Detective Tomkins! Way to go on the warrant, sir! Seriously, I apologize for that. These drivers are nuts! I am currently in pursuit of the giant ass that just passed me." He looked at the screen as the asshole was about to be revealed. "Holy shit, Tomkins! It is her! Brenda is the giant ass that just passed me!" Shae placed the light on his dashboard and accelerated.

"Listen, Scarth. Don't pursue her, please. Just follow her for now. Keep your distance. We don't want her running. I am about five minutes outside of Jackson. What is your location?"

At first there was no answer, but then there was the sound of a police siren.

"Damn it! Freaking kid!" Shae said. "Tomkins, I am in pursuit of suspect. We are passing the Wellington Reservoir on old Route 85. My speed is ninety-five, coming up to Cascade Bridge." Shae looked for Cascade Bridge on the GPS map. "I am under one minute out. Watch your speed, sprout. That bitch is liable to spike her brakes and kill you both."

Just then, Brenda's car started to slide.

"Shae, her car is sliding all over the place. I am falling back a bit."

Approaching the curve right before the bridge, Scarth

saw headlights in the other lane. The car passed his, slowed, and did a U-turn. As the car got closer, he could see it was Tomkins. Relieved with the backup, he looked back toward Brenda just in time to watch her crash through the flimsy guardrail and launch off the bridge.

By the time the detectives pulled to the side of the road and ran to the scene of the accident, three-quarters of the car was already submerged in the river.

Detective Tomkins called in two tow trucks, and the divers were en route. Shae thought about telling Joseph that he had jumped the gun in pursuing Brenda like he did, but the detective decided the world was a better, safer place without Brenda Sherrill in it.

Before the tow truck was dispatched to bring up the car, the divers investigated the wreckage. After thirty minutes, all four of them resurfaced, reporting there was no body inside the vehicle. One of the tow trucks backed up to the edge of the bridge and lowered the winch. The winch hit the water as two divers swam to it from the rocky beach beside the river. Once the car was back on the bridge, it was apparent that Brenda was not in the car.

For two days, the Jackson Police Department dragged the river, divers searched, police dogs sniffed acres surrounding the river on all sides, and helicopters searched from the sky. Brenda's body was never found. It was deemed that her body would eventually turn up, and the search was called off.

Sunday, April 3, was a sad day. Joanne woke up, put on her black mourning dress, and headed to the hospital to pick up Tom for Ruby's and Bernard's funerals. Tom had regained all memory and was fully aware of all the deaths, including Brenda's. When Joanne arrived at the hospital, Tom was waiting outside the entrance in a wheelchair. She pulled her truck up to the pickup area and helped the attendant get him into the truck. She kissed Tom on the cheek before she closed the door. The drive to the funeral was quiet.

Tom looked over at Joanne and placed her hand on top of his.

The cemetery was full of people. There had to have been three hundred or more faces, some sad, but surprisingly, most were smiling. All the kids spoke about their parents in the most loving terms. The last kid to speak was Tom. As he walked slowly to the front of his family and friends, he noticed someone standing far to the side—dressed in a black dress, a black hat, and a black veil. As he walked, the person seemed to walk along with him from afar. When he reached the pulpit, the person was gone.

Tom's eulogy was beautiful. There was not a dry eye in the crowd. He ended it by saying, "You were both right. I love you."

After two hours, many goodbyes, and dozens of white roses thrown onto both caskets, Tom and Joanne were the last two people standing over the graves of Ruby and Bernard Sherrill. Saying one last goodbye, they turned and walked toward the car, hand in hand.

They reached the car, and as they turned toward each other, they saw someone—dressed in black from head to toe—throwing something into one of the graves.

Joanne sprinted for the gravesite, and Tom followed slowly behind. By the time Tom got to the graves, Joanne was carefully climbing down onto Ruby's casket to retrieve the mysterious item the stranger had dropped.

"Oh my god!" Joanne grabbed the roots in the dirt.

As she got close to the top, Tom held out his hand. Joanne grabbed him tight, and he pulled her up the rest of the way. When she got to her feet, she dusted herself off and handed Tom the folded paper that she had retrieved from the top of Ruby's casket. It was the last Sherrill family portrait that would ever be taken.

Printed in the United States
By Bookmasters